Artificial Evil

Book 1 of The Techxorcist
by Colin F. Barnes

Colin F. Barnes's Website: www.colinfbarnes.com
Newsletter: http://eepurl.com/rFAtL

All Rights Reserved

Other Titles by Colin F. Barnes

Novels

Assembly Code: Book 2 of The Techxorcist
Annihilation Point: Book 3 of The Techxorcist

Novellas

The Daedalus Code
Dead Five's Pass

Chapter 1

City Earth, Northern Mongolia

In 2153 the lottery didn't just change lives, it ended them. And Gerry Cardle's numbers were up.

Saturday morning and Gerry should have been at home with his family. Instead, in a mood that cast its own shadow, he walked through the ten-metre-high archway to Cemprom, the largest company in City Earth.

Being at work on the weekend never seemed right. It still had a low-level hum of productivity as hundreds of drone men and women rode glass escalators and busied themselves with etiquette, but the ferocious capitalism of a weekday was stymied by the ephemeral qualities of a Saturday. They weren't really trying. It was as if the day on the calendar signalled a different mind-set. Gave them a reason to divert from their usual routine, albeit in minuscule ways. One couldn't divert too far from routine in City Earth.

The calmness appealed to him. He tried to cling to it in a vain attempt at quelling the anxiety that slithered through his nerve centre.

He approached the reception desk as usual, his suit neatly pressed by his wife, a fabric bangle around his left wrist that Marcy, his youngest daughter, made for him. Only today he was on edge. Those damned Death Lottery numbers haunted him. He shouldn't be a winner. It was impossible.

They were waiting for him in his inbox earlier that morning, flashing away in his internal mind-interface as if they were mocking him. The term 'winner' held a cruel irony that he could never get over. Still, it was just a mistake. It'd get fixed. He knew there would be some logical explanation. He just had to see his boss and sort it all out.

It wasn't right that someone like Gerry, one of the first on the exemption list, should be eligible for the D-Lottery. It must be something simple like a glitch or a bug in the system. That thought, however, was of little consolation. Gerry was the architect of the algorithm that was used to determine the 'winners', after all. If there was something wrong with the system, it was his responsibility.

How a bug could have got into the system he couldn't know. Only yesterday he and his colleagues performed a maintenance procedure on City Earth's network. It was clean.

Maybe the glitch was hidden? Someone fiddling with parts of the system on the inside. But who?

Probably Jasper. A snot-nosed, privileged automaton sent down from the Family to report on efficiency and morale, which was redundant. Like anyone displayed anything other than perfect satisfaction. The Family provided a system to cater for every whim and desire, after all. His Artificial Intelligent Assistant dutifully noted the sarcasm. No doubt he would be receiving an internal psyche report later that evening. He'd just take the report and make a virtual paper plane out of it and throw it into the trash bin, where the AIA could choke on the misfiling.

Approaching the security desk, Gerry swiped his right wrist over a small red box. Inside, a laser scanner interfaced with his ID wrist-chip and the identification routine of his AIA to generate a unique security code. Without looking at Gerry, the barely interested receptionist dictated the resulting random number to the computer.

The computer bleeped twice.

"I'm sorry, sir. You don't have access."

Gerry was already making his way past the desk with his hand out for the gate when he stopped and turned. He thought he'd misheard. He'd been through this gate hundreds of times. He looked at the receptionist, trying to tell if he was being played for a fool.

The receptionist simply pointed to the red flashing warning on the holoscreen.

"Sir, you don't have sufficient clearance. Please exit the building."

The AIA must have registered Gerry's D-Lottery status with the network already.

Gerry shook his head. Surely it had to be some kind of joke? He fully expected to see Jasper, or even his boss, giggling away in some corner. But the entrance area was empty apart from the well-groomed young man behind the desk. He sat bolt upright with perfect posture, black hair greased back in a slick, modern style. He arched a plucked eyebrow expectantly, as though he were someone important. All privilege, all class, but no skill or talent, just your typical City Earth oxygen thief—which made matters worse when oxygen was a managed resource.

"Steven, isn't it?" Gerry said. "You went to school with my eldest daughter, Caitlyn. Surely you recognise me?"

"Your ID does not have the appropriate clearance," he replied, still not engaging.

"Please. Just try again?" Gerry tugged at the bangle on his wrist, tapping his foot on the floor. Anything to remain calm, pleasant. He had to give the benefit of the doubt. The kid was just doing his job… tap, tap, tap.

Steven's tone dropped an octave. "Sir—"

"Just do it!" Gerry demanded, feeling the heat of frustration seep out of the pores on his neck and face.

Steven snorted, but tried again. "Security check: four-oh-one-three-seven-nine."

The computer beeped twice.

"Dammit, there's gotta be a mistake. Call Mike Welling. He'll vouch for me."

"That's against protocol, sir."

"Look at me. You've seen me come through these gates every day for the past month. I've worked here for over a decade. I realise your job's not to take note or pay attention, but do you think you could stop being a massive problem for just one minute and help sort this out?"

Steven turned his head like a petulant owl and spoke into his mic. "Security, please escort the guest at Gate One. He's become violent."

"Violent?" Gerry's head throbbed as if it was about to burst. The pounding of blood through veins and vessels thundered inside his skull. "You ain't seen violence, kid. Hell! You don't see anything unless it's on that damn screen."

"This episode is being recorded for criminal charges, sir."

"Call me sir one more time…"

Gerry was about to scream when he saw two security women walk down the narrow corridor to the right of the reception desk. Their expressions were stern. Jaws set and eyes focused. Gerry's heart pounded in sync with the rhythm of their loud steps as their heavy boots clattered on the Polymar floor.

One of the women wore her blonde hair in a bob cut. Her blue, augmented-reality eyes extended a couple of millimetres as she scanned Gerry. "You need to leave now, sir. Thanks for visiting Cemprom."

"Ladies, it's me, Gerry. I work here with Mike and his crew. Why can't you lot understand that?"

"Company protocol is D-Lottery protocol—"

"Check my employee stamp. Why would I have this if I didn't work here? I'm exempt!"

Gerry held out his DigiCard, which contained his security credentials, to the blue-eyed security officer.

She glimpsed at the glossy black card but didn't take it. She wasn't interested in listening to his plight. Unimpressed, she said, "D-Lottery winners are banned from this building."

"Yes, I know that. That's why I'm here on my day off. Don't you listen? What's wrong with you all?"

The other guard, with her small dark eyes, probably an ex-military spec, removed her stun-baton from her belt and took a step closer, shrouding Gerry entirely within her shadow.

Gerry snatched back his hand and balled it into a fist.

Not through any attempt at violence, but because the shakes had started. Tiny rumbles travelled across his nerve endings, making him grip his hands tight. That was the first sign of his death date being registered. His ID chip was connecting and communicating with City Earth's network.

His voice transferred the rumble as he spoke. "Please. Just call Mike Welling. He'll sort this out." Gerry stepped forward, pleading to be understood.

Too close. Too stupid. Every muscle in his body contracted—and stayed that way.

The floor rushed towards his face. His nose splattered apart on the Polymar sidewalk like a crushed cockroach. The electrical current from the stun-baton fried his nervous system, knocking him unconscious.

Chapter 2

Gerry groaned as he rolled on to his back. There was something in the air—alcohol? Couldn't be; it had never been available to the general public. Medical only. Was he in a hospital?

Something burned into the lacerations covering his nose. It had the effect of kick-starting his brain and motor functions. His hands and legs twitched.

Something hard and pointed kicked into his ribs, and a rough series of grunts hovered next to his ear. Then a man's voice... odd accent. Certainly not anything Gerry had heard before. It had a strange musical quality to it. The vowels extended, overplayed with a slight patois underlying the dialogue.

"Get up, man. You'll be impounded if ya don't move on."

Stale urine battled with the alcohol in Gerry's damaged olfactory system.

He tried to open his eyes. Resistance. He raised his hands, thankfully not closed into fists, and forced the lids open. There was something thick and warm on his fingers: blood.

Dull grey light entered his vision. That was the only

kind of light that filtered down to street level through the protective dome. Too dangerous to allow the sun to shine directly, the Family said. The Cataclysm ended hope of living in the open air anymore. Not that Gerry was old enough to know a time before the Dome—before City Earth. At thirty-five, Gerry was one of the first Future Babies: the first generation of children to be born entirely inside City Earth. He'd live to a thousand, they said. Just do as you're told, eat what you're given, drink what you're given, and listen to your AIA.

Some days Gerry wondered whether his parents weren't better off as pre-City Earth survivors. Though they'd died before they hit fifty, they'd still known what it was like before the Dome—before the control.

He blinked, clearing away the crusted blood.

He twitched his right eyeball side to side. It felt like it was submerged in treacle. The welt just above his eye from the stun-baton itched and throbbed.

Through this distorted vision, Gerry saw the shape of a man hunched over him. This person held a bottle of home brew in his fingerless gloved hand and wore a large-brimmed hat. Gerry exhaled a deep sigh. The only people who wore those kinds of hats were priests.

"Heugghhh," Gerry said. His throat was dry and unco-operative.

"Chill, man. Y'ain't gonna talk for a while. Relax, just listen."

The man leaned further into Gerry's red-cloaked vision and smiled. Dreadlocks swayed in front of his scarred face.

"Who…"

"Ya've been poezest by a devil, Gerry Cardle. But I'm

gonna get it outta ya."

Gerry tried to speak, form questions, but his throat clutched tight, his entire body bound by what seemed like a magnetic force. His muscles vibrated with fatigue, making his movements slow, painful.

The sound of a voice projected through his mind-interface interrupted his thoughts. It was Mary Magdalene: the name he gave his AIA. Mags for short.

"Good morning, Gerry. Congratulations, you're a D-Lottery winner. Your time starts now. Please ensure your personal affairs are in order and that your Last Will and Testament are filed with the City Earth Council and the Family. You'll soon receive information on funeral rates, and a counsellor will be in touch with your next of kin to finalise your arrangements. Please enjoy your last week with us. Your sacrifice is appreciated by us all."

A week left. Seven damned days. Gerry sighed. This couldn't be happening. Shouldn't be happening.

A searing wet sensation burst across his nose, making him yelp. He swiped his left arm across his chest, knocking away the gloved hand of the dread-locked pseudo-priest.

A bottle smashed onto the street.

"Ya crazy fool!" Dreads said, reaching for the bottle.

Gerry's vocal cords relaxed as he shouted, "Leave me the hell alone. Get out of here!" Energy flowed through his muscles again. His heart beat harder, pumping blood around his beaten body. He tried to get up from the gutter, but before he could stand, a gloved hand gripped his shoulder, holding him in place.

"That was 'Stem, man. It'll help ya. You understand? Ya're poezest and need my help."

"What the hell are you talking about?"

"I see it in ya code, man."

"See what? Who are you?"

"I'm ya new best friend. And I see a devil crawling through ya internal networks, switching bits, parsing code, and poking your AIA. Call me Gabe, short for Gabriel."

The man took a step back, brushed down his duster jacket, and bowed theatrically so that his dreadlocks flopped down, covering his face.

It dawned on Gerry in an instant. This was no priest. He noticed the triangular dots of scar tissue on his neck and the embedded chromed pin sockets in his temples. Even those mad staring eyes gave it away: hacker, burned-out, crazy hacker. He'd obviously lost his mind—got too deep into code, lost touch with reality. But how did he know about his D-Lottery numbers? Gerry had only found out himself earlier that morning.

Gerry noticed something odd: his dermal wrist implant was now flashing. Embedded into its flat square fascia was a tiny red dot the size of a pinhead. A thin concentric circle of blood surrounded the dot: a sign of a security breach.

"You've hacked me?"

"I had to see what's inside ya. And trust me. Ya code is in bad shape, man."

"I… what… you…" Gerry couldn't find the words. He'd been violated, his internal systems poked at. So wrong, so… unnatural. The consequences were unimaginable.

Gerry struck out a fist, but Gabe caught his feeble attempt.

"Relax, man. Just come with me, and I'll explain every-thing. We ain't gotta lot of time. Security'll be sweeping any minute."

Gerry shrugged his hand away and promptly wobbled side to side, still dazed from the stun-baton. He tried to fling out a fist or a foot, anything to strike Gabe, but the exertion was too much. He leaned over and vomited.

With his head down, he started to pitch forward as the dizziness overwhelmed him.

Gabe caught him, pulling him upright.

Giving in, Gerry allowed himself to be led away. At the very least he could wait until there was somewhere to rest and then figure it all out. It was still morning. The street was deserted. Tall buildings freshly cleaned and devoid of dirt or any signs of industry lined each side. They seemed to loom inwards almost accusingly. Everywhere was just so perfect, and Gerry had spoiled the place. A pang of guilt welled up in his stomach when he looked at the ugly patch of liquids on the floor. He hated littering. It never took much effort to look after one's surroundings. Vomiting one's breakfast on the floor was not the behaviour of a good citizen.

Behind the guilt something gnawed at him: regret. He'd left too much of himself behind, too much DNA.

"Where are you taking me?"

"Just chill, man. We're gonna fix ya right up. We're gonna exorcise ya."

Gerry had no clue what he was getting into. He had no strength to protest. Besides, a security patrol vehicle had made its way up the road. A grey and blue box—the colours of City Earth's security force, two square metres in size, hovered with a low whine, powered by a hydrogen fuel cell and vertical take-off and lift, VTOL, engine. A series of

LEDs flashed red and blue along its side. It stopped, and a small floodlight illuminated the scene of the broken bottle and puddle of puke. A robotic arm with a swab on the end took a sample. His DNA would now be registered as a criminal. No jury needed. Bang to rights.

It was the least of his concerns. The D-Lottery would kill him within a week anyway.

Gabe dragged him down the street and round the corner.

Gerry lost his bearings after a few short minutes. These unfamiliar streets seemed more foreboding and darker than his upper-class district, but then Gerry rarely ventured into the communal zones. Had no reason too, either, being one of the Cemprom's most gifted algorithm designers. Only the top echelons for him. He'd no choice now, though. Had to get word to his family, find Mike, and sort out this D-Lottery nonsense. The consequences of a compromised algorithm were beyond anything he'd contemplated before. City Earth's systems and networks were rock solid. Impenetrable. Until now.

"Ya've got some bad mojo in ya, man," Gabe said.

"Yeah? No shit."

***

Gerry's escort stopped him in front of a rough wooden door, waved his hand over the lock. It chirped, and a small clunk sounded. The door swung open, casting a wide beam of golden light onto the dull street. A pair of brass-rimmed goggles with darkened lenses appeared in the gap. They gave the fragile girl wearing them the countenance of a nervous lemur. She wore her hair in a bright pink Mohican with complicated, almost filigree style tattoos on the side of her head.

"Petal, I found him," Gabe said.

The goggled girl checked both sides of the street and then stood aside to let them enter.

She was young and twitchy in her synthetic leather trousers and a fitted faux biker jacket. Her lips were tattooed bright purple. It always amazed Gerry how these young girls could put up with the pain. There were few countercultures in City Earth. Most were tame as the citizens wouldn't, or didn't want to, rebel against the norm. It mostly extended to a slightly different hair style or basic modifications to clothes.

He'd never seen a girl like this before. She screamed rebellion, danger. He was quickly getting out of his comfort zone. As he passed her, she cocked her head to one side, assessing him. He wondered what was behind the goggles. The thought intrigued and scared him in equal measure. Without seeing her eyes, it was difficult to read her intentions. What was she thinking? What did she think about him?

"Go through to the back, Gez," she said quietly. "Don't touch a thing."

Her voice almost sang to him such was the lightness. The vowels had a slight rough edge to them, making her sound alien to him. It didn't have the clear pseudo-English accent that everyone within the Dome had. Where did she and Gabe come from? He'd never met anyone within the City who spoke so differently, which brought up a series of questions that he didn't, or couldn't dwell on.

Inside, the room was far grander than what Gerry had expected from the grim aspect of the exterior. Panelled wood, probably mahogany, lined the walls. Expensive. Wood was so rare and to use it as wall decoration was so— the words escaped him.

"Careless? Vulgar?" she asked him.

"Wait, you can read my mind?"

"Nah, you're on the network. Your AIA's freaking out, spraying like a panicked skunk. Don't worry. It's secure here." Her goggles switched from opaque to clear, revealing glossy black eyes, reflecting Gerry's face like mirrored spheres. He caught himself staring, falling.

"I can see your code. It's grim. You're in a world of trouble." Her head twitched.

Gerry blinked, looked away, and gripped the sides of his throbbing head. He reached into his jacket pocket. Empty.

"Where's my comm?"

"Smashed to bits. Your security peeps crushed it when they kicked you out."

"Great. Can I use yours?"

"Off the grid. Don't have one."

"Your network? I just need to get word to a friend. He can sort out this D-Lottery nonsense. And then you can let me go. I've got family. I'm—"

"Exempt?" Gabe said. "Aye, should be, but a devil got inside ya and messed with ya algorithm. And ya can't go transmitting out onto the main network. Way too dangerous."

"How the hell do you know all this? Just tell me straight. Who are you people?"

The girl spoke up. "We're specialists of a sort. A little

bit off the beaten track. We slip through the cracks in the system. We tracked a demon right here in the City. In you, and in your pal Mike."

"He's here? He's okay?"

"Um... he's kinda dead," Petal said.

"Mike? Dead? No. This can't be. You're lying. Surely!"

Petal and Gabe stood watching, stony-faced.

Gerry hoped this was all just a lie or some kind of big elaborate joke. Mike was like that, always playing pranks, but would he go this far? It was funny, sure, about the D-Lottery numbers, but not for this long, and these freaks? Maybe they killed him, and he was next. A billion thoughts bloomed into life and expired almost instantly. He tried to access the logic portion of Mags, but she didn't respond. Probably occupied with informing the various official channels of his imminent demise. They'd need cover at work. His daughters would need a new father figure. And then there was his wife, Beth. She would need a new husband. The family unit was an important part of City Earth's society. It was how things worked.

A part of Gerry knew Beth wouldn't be terribly upset. Their relationship, for whatever reason, was never particularly intimate. She had a 'defined role in the family unit' and was apparently happy with that. Still, it didn't make it hurt any less.

Turning back to them and trying to focus, Gerry said, "So tell me, what happened to Mike?"

"He's out back," Gabe said. "Wanna see?"

Gerry wasn't sure if he did. All the time there was no physical evidence there was a chance this was all a massive misunderstanding—a nightmare.

"Come through, Gez," Petal said. "You'll see."

"Is it bad?"

"It's a little screwed up, to be honest." Her goggles returned to their inky opaqueness.

Petal took Gerry by the hand and led him through an open doorway into a clinical kitchen: compact and barely large enough for four people. The cabinets and worktops were the usual self-clean white alloy.

As he ducked under the low door frame, he noticed masses of wire mesh running through the ceiling from room to room. Shielding perhaps? Or a Faraday cage of sorts? That probably explained the security of their internal network.

The kitchen smelled of alcohol. Numerous antique glass bottles were lined up on a wooden table. Next to them was an alloy container—about a half-metre square—filled with a writhing black liquid.

Petal must have seen his confusion. "NanoStem solution. Similar to the stuff that Gabe used to heal your facial wound. This one we've impregnated with defence nodes. It's liquid virus protection. Cool, huh?"

Gerry didn't know what to think. He just worked with numbers, factors, and probabilities.

Underneath the stench of booze, something rotten hung in the air. A putrefied, sweet smell tingled his nose hairs and stuck in the back of his throat.

Petal walked to a nook and opened a curtain. Sitting on his ass was Mike Welling. His skin had mulched to a grey-green mottled colour, as if it had rotted from the inside out. It sagged in disgusting black and purple lumps. He sat in a pool of black viscous liquid that dripped from every orifice—the NanoStem solution.

"You can see we've been trying to help him. For two days we managed to keep it out, but last night the demon breached the 'Stem defence, and… well, you can see the results. It's a particularly brutal one."

Waves of grief flashed through Gerry's guts. His legs felt like rubber. He grabbed the edge of the table to support himself. "You're mad. You're all bloody mad."

"That's possible, my friend, but ya need us," Gabe said from the doorway. "That thing there is ya pal Mike. That's what's gonna happen to ya. It hacked Mike's AI first, changed the exemption list, and has chosen ya for poezession. Y'ain't got long, man."

"I don't feel… Mags hasn't changed. Nothing's bypassed my security."

"Not yet," Petal said. "But you feel those shakes?"

Gerry nodded. "That's just Mags doing her thing with the D-Lottery reg."

"No. That's the demon screwing the bejesus out of your Mags's back door. It's trying to impregnate her like it's done with your pal Mike. Here, watch."

Petal pushed Gerry closer to the zombified creature that barely resembled his old friend and boss. They'd known each other since they were toddlers. Came out of the same breeding programme. Selected for the same career path. Gerry had always looked up to him, and here he was, a shell. A rotting shell.

He blinked the tears from his eyes, breathed deeply— and then regretted it. He gagged on the stench of bad eggs and rotting meat.

Petal took a HackSlate from her breast pocket and

swiped a three-fingered gesture across its neon-blue holographic surface. The device was barely larger than her palm and as thin as paper. She was connecting to their internal network. Gerry had heard about these devices. A few of his colleagues had worked on defence systems against them. They had the ability to bypass most frontline security systems. He'd have to ask her where they got them from, but now wasn't the time.

Petal smiled at Gerry. Her full lips stretched wide, exposing sharp canines. She resembled a wolf pup on the edge of adulthood.

"Time to wake him up." She drew yet more complex gestures across the slate until a few seconds later the body twitched. "Hey, Mike. Your old pal's here to say hi."

Zombie Mike lifted its head, focusing a milky eye on Gerry. A flash of recognition slithered across its vision. Its swollen lips parted, and it spoke.

"Kill. Me. Kill me now…" And then the thing started to thrash against the restraints before a different voice spoke. "Ahhh, Mr Cardle, just the man I was sent to get—what treasures you'll give to me… what secrets you'll reveal. Now, come here!" The thing lurched towards Gerry, trying to claw at him, but the restraints held it back.

Gerry jumped back. "Oh, god, Mike!" Gerry screamed, shocked, unable to comprehend the horror of the situation. The thing moaned, then whined, seemingly in pain. "Can't you put him out of his misery?"

"We're tryin', man." Gabe pointed to the NanoStem solution. "The demon has royally screwed with his AIA. Got into his brain, neural pathways, nervous system. It's like a living virus. An artificial evil. You guys, with ya goddamn brain-mods, are clueless as to what ya've done. It's using him to get to the algorithm in ya head, in ya damned AIA."

Gerry ignored the AIA argument. He'd monitored the anti-AIA groundswell for years, but the Family always handled it. Severe punishments for those who uninstalled them soon quelled the rebellion. And despite his wondering what it'd be like without a modded brain, there wasn't a single report of anything detrimental to having one. He turned to Petal. "Have you tried—"

"Everything. Apart from one."

"And you need me for this one thing?"

"Yeah."

"And it's dangerous?"

"Hell yeah."

Chapter 3

Mike Welling, Gerry's best friend, colleague, and godfather to his kids, was now essentially the animated dead. Before this moment, Gerry had never given a second thought to anything paranormal. Heck, no one did these days. Technology was so prevalent and life so comfortable that there was no need to seek solace in superstition, myth or religion. There were still a tiny minority of people, usually the crazed or the high, who believed in such things, but generally that kind of old-fashioned faith had died decades ago.

But seeing that thing, that creature in the corner, made Gerry think twice. There was something not right about the situation, about Gabe, the girl, any of it. How did he end up smack-bang in the middle of it all? Coincidence was the usual explanation. But maybe there was some other reason? He wasn't sure about anything anymore. Gerry took one last look at the forlorn, animated doppelgänger and returned to the living room.

Gabe and Petal said nothing as he walked past them.

He slumped into a sofa.

Gabe sat opposite. His eyes were deep set and surrounded by a thin blanket of veined skin. Gerry noticed he was the self-medicating kind. The telltale red blotches across his nose gave it away. But after seeing what he had to deal with, Gerry was beginning to understand.

"We tracked the demon for a week before it got into ya boss," Gabe said. "We tried to stop it, but it was too quick for either of us. It's using Mike's AIA."

"That's why it's keeping Mike alive?"

"He's not alive, not really. There's nothing of Mike left in there. His mind's been shot to hell. The demon just wanted him for his AIA and the resulting access. We believe the algorithm's been the target all along."

"But why?"

"You should know that. It's your algorithm that determines the D-Lottery numbers."

Gerry considered the ramifications. What would a seemingly evil force want with the exemption list? People could be added or removed. What would be the benefit of taking people off the list and altering the algorithm?

"Oh no…"

"What is it, man? Tell me."

Gerry wondered if this is what it felt like to go to confession back in the days before the Dome. "I control the algorithm, right? The buck stops with me, now that Mike's—well, you know…" He still couldn't believe he was dead; he tried to compartmentalise his grief into a neat and tidy box. Some of it inevitably spilled out, but he regained control after a few deep breaths.

"Go on," Gabe prompted.

"The members of the Family and the controlling councils are on the exemption list. If they are removed and this demon or whatever it is can change the algorithm, it can choose whose numbers come up, and the network will do the rest."

"By 'do the rest', you mean kill 'em? Because of your goddamn interconnections and reliance on the network?"

"Yes, but damn it, how can it change the algorithm? Only through me and my systems at Cemprom can that be changed. And besides, the councils and the Family are ring-fenced from the algorithm anyway."

"The code's messed up. Somehow, through Mike, it's able to get in somewhere. There's a leak in ya security. Cemprom, and by extension you, have been compromised."

"Without me knowing? Impossible. It's all a part of me, damn it." That violated feeling again spread its icy fingers through his brain. Then he remembered—his dermal implant. "You! You hacked me! How do I know all this wasn't you? You could have put the demon or whatever it is in my code."

Gabe just shook his head. "I needed to check ya code, man. How many instances of a hacked AIA via a dermal implant have you ever heard of?"

Gerry thought for a second and knew it was impossible. But the alternative was a demon AI on the loose in the network? No way. It was unheard of. He snorted out the remaining air in his lungs. His temples throbbed. "Okay. Let's assume you're right. Why is it waiting a week for the network to kill me when it could just end me now?"

"Who said it would wait?"

The shadow cast from the wide-brimmed hat grew darker over Gabe's eyes. His already deathly pallor deepened. The consequences of that question played out in

Gerry's mind: if the demon already had control of his AIA, then he wasn't needed. He could be killed—at any time.

"I need to contact my family."

Gabe shook his head. "It ain't safe. Ya can't speak with 'em again."

"What? Ever?"

Gabe sighed and stood up. A multitude of creaks and clicks came from his joints. It was obvious not being in the network excluded him from the Medicaid provisions afforded to regular members of society.

"The demon will keep ya alive for however long it considers you an asset—like it's done with Mike."

"Which could mean I'm done for any second."

"Not completely. Not yet, anyway. Come with me. We'll get ya hooked up to the network and see what's crawling around inside ya. This is what Petal and I do. Have a little faith, man."

***

The room behind the curtain resembled a grey cube with several old-fashioned computer terminals set into darkened nooks along the walls. Gerry recognised them from his parents' photographs of their lives before the Cataclysm.

"I can't believe any of these survived," he said out loud, more for his comfort than general interest. The place stank of sweat and mould. A high-back swivel chair sat in front of each cubicle. All chrome curves and angles, with heavy straps integrated in the arms. Not a good sign. He'd heard about underground sex dens, but since the full integration of the city-wide network, that kind of thing was quickly snuffed out. He'd even worked on some of the search strings and algorithms to identify the chatter and thought patterns via people's AIAs.

Overhead, running along the ceiling, more wire mesh writhed between joists. He could sense the flow of petabytes that ran through the fibre-optic cables. A part of him wanted to dive in the current of information. See what flowed there. See what could be manipulated, assessed, controlled.

"This network is secure, right?"

"As secure as it gets," Petal said, with not a hint of exaggeration in her soft voice.

In front of the computer monitors, a series of cables with interface plugs lay like entwined snakes.

It was the ultimate crime to access one's AIA so directly. And to do it off-the-grid, on a secure network, was akin to screwing an AIDS-riddled prostitute with no protection. Potential suicide.

Gerry's skin crawled, and a cold spot spread throughout his spine. This was up there with blatant satanic worship or treason.

"This the only way?"

"Let's just get a move on before you snuff it, eh?" Petal pushed him towards a chair.

No other options. Who knew how long he had? Could be struck down at any time. The dermal implants were fitted with concentrated Cyanide+ V2.0. All controlled by the AIA, of course—and by extension the Family. Guaranteed one thousand years of life—if you did what they wanted.

This was not what they wanted.

But he had other responsibilities: Beth, his wife, and his two girls. He thought about them. They needed him. He needed them. He had to do something. He couldn't face the thought of not being there for his family.

Closing his eyes, he uttered, "Okay."

Gerry mentally transferred his PIN. He was interfacing with Mags. It didn't feel like it used to. Felt foreign. It responded like it should, but Gerry knew something had changed. A silence of data chatter. A neurotic silence full of tension, and expectation.

He requested a rundown of his inbox. Nothing.

Checked his social networks. Nothing.

Searched his personal net for the latest news headlines. Nothing.

The demon broke down each node as it got closer to its destination.

Mags accepted Gerry's PIN, and he was at root level.

Gerry turned to Gabe and Petal.

"Okay. Do what you got to do."

Gerry's arms thrashed against the restraints in the chair, and his body tensed like a rod: every fibre of his being rejected the process, but it didn't stop. He thought he would experience something special, something enlightening. Mags had been a part of him for as long as he could remember, and he had a certain image of her sitting on a grand throne, tentacles manipulating computer terminals, but he saw nothing. He felt a great deal, though. A pain in the soul was the only way he could describe it.

"She's been busy," Gabe said, staring at the old CRT monitor inside his cubicle opposite Gerry.

"Poor girl got penetrated," Petal said.

"Does it have control of her?" Gerry asked.

"Not yet. That's the good news. Bad news is the demon's got its claws into her."

"The algorithm? Does it have full access?"

"I can't see that far in," Gabe said. "Petal, what can ya see?"

"The demon is using Mike's AIA to interface with yours, Gerry. It's screwing by proxy. Did you bridge your systems for some reason?"

Gerry thought back. "Damn it. Yes. Last week. We were experimenting with a new internode protocol. It was done entirely off the network, though. Nothing could have..." Then he thought of Jasper again. He'd started work just a day before.

"How can we stop it?"

Silence.

All three sat in the darkened room, strapped into the chairs, heads jacked into the local network. Their bodies acted as nothing more than servers and routers. Humanity was in short supply.

"Guys, just tell me. I doubt I've got long if it's screwing with the algorithm."

"You've got kids, right?" Gabe asked.

"Yeah, two girls."

"A wife?" Petal asked.

"A wife, yes."

"If you want to see them again, you need to open your AIA ports to the demon. Let it in entirely."

Gerry wanted to turn and stare at the girl, to give her his best 'are you mentally ill?' look, but the restraints held.

Gabe spoke up and broke the harsh silence. "Once we have it in your AIA, we can trap it 'ere in our protection room."

"And how do I do that?" Gerry asked.

"Hang on. I'm sniffing it and will tell you the port numbers to open up. It'll jump in quicker than a hobo at a free food store."

Pulses of information threatened to fry Gerry's brain as Petal let down some of the walls of protection. The demon's digital tentacles were all over Mags, searching for entry. Her subroutines launched into action but were instantly uninstalled by the demon. This made Gerry's head twitch as if he were having a fit. His eyes fluttered in a frenzied motion. He wanted to call out, tell her to stop, but then he heard Petal's voice over the communicator.

"Eighty-oh-one. Thirty-three-zero. Seventy-oh-eight-seven."

Gerry heard a harsh feedback screech through his communicator, followed by the bizarrely calm voice of Gabe. "Good work, Petal. Punch those numbers, man. Let the beast in, and I'll do the rest."

Gerry's hands thrashed uncontrollably against the arm rests. Jolts of pain mixed with overwhelming feelings of doom crashed through his system. He'd never experienced evil until this point. That thought caught him off-guard. Was it evil? It was just code, just another artificial-intelligence programme. Surely evil couldn't be programmed...?

Ignoring this random thought process, he transferred the instructions to Mags to open the specified ports. It was easier than expected. No resistance, no warnings.

Petal was right. The demon was quick. The nanosecond

the ports opened, that black mass entered Mags like an eager teenager beginning their first sexual experience.

There was no struggle, no last dump of security subroutines. It was quite the anticlimax. Gerry had expected something more explosive. Mags remained silent, running its various processes as normal: no reports, no alarms, no execution of disaster protocols or breach of defence systems.

"Did it work?" Gerry asked between panting breaths.

There was a long silence. Gerry could feel the tension in the room. Petal was unusually quiet. Gabe was busy at work, he knew that much. He could see in his mind the flow of traffic increase exponentially from Gabe's terminal to his AIA.

After five minutes of furious typing, grunts and expletives. Gabe finally spoke. "It's done."

"Now what?" Gerry asked.

"I exorcise it. Ya need to get off the grid, though. Uninstall Mags completely."

"Are you mad?"

"Possibly, yeah, but trust me on this one."

"But if I uninstall her, I'll—"

"Be a free man? Absolutely. It's that or death—for you and for anyone else connected with you."

"My whole life will be over. I'll be a criminal, a rogue. My whole existence, and my family's, is on the grid. I can't do that. I'll be—"

"Just like us," Petal said.

Mags communicated to him, *"Thank you for your sacrifice, Gerry. You have just one day left. Please inform the Council of your funeral arrangements."*

"It's changed ya internal clock, man. The algorithm's next. Think about ya contact list. Everyone on that list could have their numbers up. Ya family, friends, colleagues. Is it worth it?"

Gerry considered Gabe's words while trying to ignore that he potentially had just one day left to live. Going off the grid was almost as bad as dying. He would lose the ability to work, to support his family. He'd be an outlaw.

He would have to leave his family behind. His entire life as he knew it would be over. The alternative was either death or this demon taking entire sections of society off the exemption list. Too much to risk. How could he willingly allow that to happen? His city, the only place he'd ever known, was precious. It was a virtual utopia—for good or bad—and he couldn't just idly watch its destruction, regardless of the downsides.

Not much of a choice, though: his own life and an end to his suffering, or possibly an entire city's stability. As difficult as it was, he realised in truth it was an easy decision when he thought about it: he couldn't let the whole city down. Sure, the place had problems. The Family were maniacal with their control, but people still had good lives, safe lives.

The image of his daughters and wife conjured in his mind. He couldn't let them suffer if he had the choice to stop it. Picturing them that morning around the breakfast table, he ignored the pain that stabbed at his heart and made the decision. He logged in at super-root level, meaning he could access the parts of his AIA that controlled how it worked at a fundamental level. It wasn't something anyone could do.

He'd realised he had this ability while testing potential exploits at Cemprom. During the experimentation, he'd created a secret login procedure to his AIA, mostly out of curiosity. Like everyone in the city, he had no desire to leave the network. But this time he had a damned good reason.

Once logged in, he activated a piece of code that, as far as he knew, no one had executed before. He was just a few seconds away from living without the essential life support of the network.

Gerry closed his eyes, squeezed in the tears. Hesitated.

"Do it, man, do it now!" Gabe said.

"Let her go, Gez," Petal added. "Let her fly."

He could feel the colossal blackness manipulating Mags, trying to log him out. Trying to prevent him from entering the fatal code. But he was at the base. Nothing could stand in the way of his release, the cease of support, the release of society, of being one of many.

Using his mind-interface, he moved a cursor over a representation of a door with 'EXIT' marked on its surface. All he had to do was open the door and walk his avatar out. The AIA would be uninstalled. The demon would no longer be in charge of his destiny. Mags would be free to exist in her limited silicon shell. Without a human to assist, he wondered what she would do. Just how much independent thought did they have?

He closed his eyes and concentrated on the interface. The door remained closed. It shrank and moved to the right of his view. A grid of thumbnail images of his family replaced it, and he scrolled through each one. He attempted to burn their happy, smiling faces into his brain. He would no longer be able to carry them with him once Mags was gone.

He cried uncontrollably.

Tears flowed down his face like small pebbles down a hill. Each image blinked out of view. The demon. It was wiping the photographs—his memories!

He reached out and gripped the handle of the symbolic door and pushed it open. Bright light flooded into his interface, and a cautionary paragraph of text hovered into view. It was the usual stuff: *This process is not reversible... are you sure you wish to delete... criminal offence punishable by death...*

He mentally marked the agreement checkbox and clicked OK. Nothing would ever be okay again. Never seeing his family was not okay. Never working at Cemprom with his now dead buddy Mike was not okay.

And then he was cut loose. Just a regular human again—whatever that meant.

He held his breath, expecting something different, expecting to somehow feel strange, as though his previous life was lived vicariously through his AIA. But he was the same old Gerry.

Then it hit him like a hammer: he could never return home. That's what felt different: the detachment. A wave of loneliness coursed through him like a strong wind whipping through his clothes. He felt nauseous again and wanted to sleep, to dream, to pretend none of it happened.

But the breathing, corporeal bodies of Gabe and Petal sitting next to him in their individual cubicles reminded him that he could dream all he wanted. He would never be the same again.

Chapter 4

Gabriel spun round in his chair. "Good job, man. We'll do our bit next. Just relax for a bit, yeah?"

"Yeah. Relax. I'll crack a cold beer while I'm at it." They weren't listening. Gabe and Petal were chattering away about stuff Gerry had never heard of before. He just watched, fascinated, as they blended these old tools with current-day technology like modern-day alchemists.

"Demon's big," Petal said.

"I'm containing it now. Ya ready for download?" Gabe asked the girl, swirling round in his chair. The multitude of snakes plugged into his brain wrapped and tangled behind him.

"Yeah, give it to me."

Petal typed furiously at a beige, retro QWERTY keyboard, and her screen monitor flashed with lines of computer code. It was real old. Gerry remembered something about that language in his college days. It was antiquated then, but now it was positively dead. Very low level, almost chip level, which was unheard of now. Outdated symbols: hashes, colons, dashes, dollar signs, and various brackets filled lines on the screen.

Petal's head thrashed side to side, and she stopped

typing. Her goggles turned blood red. She screamed a piercing note of extreme agony.

Gerry leapt out of his chair towards her, but the cables attached to his neck halted his movement with a crack. He crumpled to the floor.

"Leave her, man. She's containing it," Gabe said from across the room.

"What are you doing?"

"Exorcising the AI."

Gerry turned to look at Gabe's screen, expecting the same code, but instead he saw proper words, old words. He managed to read just a few before Petal screamed and thrashed violently again.

From his limited knowledge of religion—he only had a part of an antique bible, which belonged to his mother—it seemed like a sermon of sorts. Gabe was actually typing biblical commands to the demon, a piece of code, albeit an artificially intelligent piece of code. That idea raised its head again: had someone coded evil?

Minutes of frantic typing from Gabe and screaming from Petal stretched Gerry's nerves to the snapping point. Sweat dripped from Gabe's face as he hunched over the keyboard, banging out word after word after word. The screams reached a crescendo and finally died. Gabe collapsed into his chair, wiped the sweat from his brow, and turned to Gerry.

"It's done." Gabe pulled the cables from the sockets in his head and rushed over to Petal, who slouched low in her chair.

Gerry unwound himself from the snake nest of cables and moved quickly to the chair. He and Gabe stood either side and looked down at the fragile thing that was once the full-of-bravado Petal.

Her goggles were opaque again, and blood dripped from her lip.

Gerry moved his hand to her pale neck to check for a pulse. Her chest was still; she resembled a corpse.

A delicate hand reached out, weak fingers encircled his wrist.

"Don't," Petal said, her voice cracking.

The tip of her tongue escaped the tight aperture of her purple lips and licked at the blood before darting back in.

"This one's salty," she said quietly, her breath shallow. "Like pretzels."

"Pretzels?" asked Gerry.

Petal turned her face to Gerry and pulled the goggles off her face. Her eyes were no longer the shiny black orbs from before. Gerry was silent. Fixated. Her eyes glowed scarlet, like LEDs. He couldn't even make out her pupils. Something swirled inside.

"Beautiful, ain't they?" Gabe said.

"What are you?"

"I can do some strange things. My eyes are like this because it's the manifestation of the things I contain. You'll get used to it, eventually. The effects aren't always the same. It's pretty cool, right?"

"You're containing the demon code inside you? Isn't that—"

"Look, we ain't got much time. We need to leave town and dispose of it," Gabe said.

"How do you do this? Is it some kind of new tech, or…"

"Petal's special," Gabe said. "She's disconnected from

City Earth's grid like me and, of course, you now, but she's her own special kind of ring-fenced network. Ain't that right, girl?"

"Yeah, I ain't the same kind of hacker like Gabe here. I'm impervious to data. I can kinda block code demons, bad AIs, and viruses inside me, like a secure safe house for bad code. But when I get full, like now, I need to dump 'em somewhere safe. And we need your help."

"What do you need?"

"To get out of the city," Gabe said.

Gerry choked on spit and wanted to laugh. "Are you both completely insane? No one gets out of the city. There's nothing out there!"

"Oh, Gez." Petal patted him on his head. "You've got so much to learn. Don't worry, though. You'll pick it up as we go along."

"Pick what up?"

"You're one of us now. You're gonna work with us. And you kinda owe us for saving your life."

"Yeah, but, what—"

Petal stood up and disconnected her cables. She pulled her goggles back down.

She leant into his ear, real close. He could smell something sweet on her breath: a perfume of sorts. Her lips brushed his ear as she spoke. "You're a Techxorcist now, Gez. You're gonna help us track and contain our next target."

"What target?"

Gabe turned to face Gerry.

"A particularly nasty AI that's gunning for President Kuznetski. It's already breached City Earth's outer network. It'll get to him in a matter of days. It came on the coattails of yours. It's much more complex, though. Real evil. But first we need to empty Petal's internal storage. We leave in five minutes."

"What does this other AI want? Who's behind it?"

"That's what we're gonna find out, man. We've stuck a trace on it for now."

"Shouldn't we just alert City security? At least let me get in touch with Cemprom. Tell them what happened to Mike. They've got good hackers there. They can—"

Gabe shook his head. "Nothing goes in or out, ya hear? I suspect it's an inside job. We can't risk it. We'll nuke it before it gets to him, and then we'll see what's what."

President Miralam Kuznetski, a grandson of a Croatian diplomat, was one of the first proper immigrants to the City. The Family brought him in due to his heritage and his father's support of the Family during World War III. Although he portrayed himself as an independent leader, guiding the City Earth Council for the benefit of the citizens, he'd often tried to dictate the direction of Cemprom's research.

Although Gerry didn't trust him, he was still the appointed helmsman of the City, and stability was important. If he was taken out, affected by the AI, the ramifications could run through every department of the City.

***

Gerry sat alone in the drawing room, his head swirling with confusion. It was all moving so fast. He thought about his family. No doubt they would find out soon enough about his numbers and go through the formalities of a ceremony. There'd be no burial without a body.

He would have to get word to them soon, somehow. But even that would jeopardise their safety. The Family didn't like loose ends and would interrogate them to find his whereabouts. It would be much better if they didn't know the truth or have any trail that could lead to him, which, of course, meant entire network silence. He'd have to do it by proxy somehow.

"You're gonna need this." Gabe dropped an aged leather duffel bag at his feet.

The top fell open, and Gerry pulled out the contents: two books, a vial of NanoStems, and a polished brass and mahogany box.

"This was my old man's. I don't use it no more." Gabe motioned to the box.

Gerry opened the lid and gasped at its contents.

"A pistol? How did you—"

"No time for more chatter. Just take the gun, and read the books on the way."

Petal arrived in the doorway between the drawing room and kitchen. "Nice, ain't it? Ammo's in the bag."

"Lighter than I thought it would be." Gerry lifted the gun, feeling its weight in his hand.

"You know Helix++?" she asked.

"I'm familiar with it." Gerry lifted up the heavy paper tome titled *Programming Exploits and Malicious Algorithms with Helix++.*

"Transport's on its way. Let's get out of Dodge. Security detail's tracked our general location. They're like a swarm of angry wasps. Won't be long before they find this place.

Besides, I've only got a couple of hours."

"Until what?" Gerry asked.

"To get rid of the demon. It's a big'un, and it's already passed my internal security. It'll be out in a few hours if we don't dump it."

"Out where? Code can't just float about in the air."

"The Meshwork," Petal said. "You government types don't know about that, do you?" Petal gave him a sly grin. "It's all around us, Gez. We act as nodes. You do too, now. You're basically an Internet switch. A hyperintelligent, bad-ass switch. You just don't know it yet. But you will."

Gerry ignored the dig and minor revelation. He'd enough to think about without digging into yet more underground tech. He'd figure it all out eventually. "If this demon AI did get 'out', can't you just recontain it?"

"Not really, and we're risking all the other stuff escaping. We're talking about a mass prison break of biblical proportions here, Gez, and there's some bad mojo in me right now that we really would prefer stayed tightly locked away. Besides, it took a crap-load of effort to win those contracts and get payment. If we lose 'em now, all our bins won't be worth a damn."

"Bins?"

"Currency. Digital coinage," Gabe said. "Outside of ya fancy little utopia, the rest of us have to have something to use to exchange resources. Those of us off-the-grid don't get nothing for free. Besides, ya gonna earn us a pretty penny with your skills. Ya just need to trust in 'em. So, ya ready?"

Gerry couldn't find the words. He tried to remember how to use his real brain to sort through all these new terms, data sets, and ramifications. It would take a while to not be able to manipulate an AIA, but he felt excited, and worried, and anxious. Like being a teenager learning the rules and boundaries the hard way.

"Don't think I've got much choice, then, do I?"

"Sure ya've got a choice, man. Ya can join us and do something good. Put your skills to use. Or ya can walk out that door and let the security deal with ya."

Petal looked at the thick watch on her wrist. "Shake a leg, princess. I meant it when I said seriously bad mojo will go down if I don't dump these demons."

"I just want to do one more thing before we go."

Before Gabe and Petal had a chance to say anything, Gerry walked through the kitchen and approached the mewling, zombie Mike.

"I'm sorry, pal. Take care in the afterlife. If there is one."

Gerry jumped at the surprisingly loud crack from the gunshot. The head exploded as if it were a ripe pumpkin. Brains and blood smothered the back wall of the nook, and the lumpy body slumped forward. This time it remained still.

Gerry looked back at Petal and Gabe. Petal flashed him another wolfish grin. Gabe's eyes grew wide with surprise. They clearly underestimated him. Good. It was best to keep them from knowing too much. They'd have to wait to find out what he was really capable of.

"Let's go flush these demons, then. The quicker we get out, the quicker I can get back to my family." He wasn't sure if that was entirely possible. But right now, he'd cling to anything to avoid admitting it was completely hopeless.

Petal and Gabe glanced at each other briefly, sharing an

unspoken message, before filling a backpack with bottles of water and food rations sealed in vacuum graphene foil from the kitchen cabinets. Gabe took the pack and headed to a section of the wall inside an alcove opposite Mike's corpse.

Pushing against a particular area, Gabe stood back as the wall moved inwards, revealing a dark gap.

Petal took Gerry's elbow and beckoned him to follow Gabe down a flight of stairs.

As they descended, it occurred to Gerry that these weren't regular stairs. They were motionless escalators. They were heading into an old, disused subway station. The smell of carbon dust and body odour clung to the air still.

The three of them stood on the platform, waiting.

Gerry was about to ask how they would leave the City when a rush of air and whirr of electric motors answered it for him.

"A train? Are you guys for real?"

Gabe grinned at him. "Man, there's so much you don't know."

"Tell me about it," Gerry said, trying to stop his mind from spinning as each perception of the world was stripped away like an onion skin. "How is this even possible? I thought all these kinds of vehicles were out of action since the Cataclysm?"

"The Family like you to believe that everything was destroyed," Petal said. "They wanna make you think it all begins and ends with the Dome, but it don't. There's a world out there, Gez. It's messed up, dangerous, exciting and a hundred other things, but it ain't empty."

"How do they even allow this to run?"

"What makes ya think they even know about it?" Gabe said. "Listen, man, they built this city on top of an existing town. An old traditional Mongolian town that was on the up-and-up. A few transport links here, a few developments there. You get the idea. But when the war finished and they built the Dome, they left a few relics here, like this train and the tunnel."

"But how is it running?"

"Hackers, engineers, people with a vested interest in staying off the grid," Petal said. "This old train line was still connected to the power grid. It took just a little bit of modification on our part to reroute the signals so that they wouldn't notice the power usage."

Gerry looked at the fuse box on the side of the stairwell. The case hung open, and various wires rose from the electronics and snaked up into the ceiling, where a number of tiles hung loose. "They must know," Gerry said, not believing this could be going on under the Family's nose.

"Not this, they don't," Petal added. "But don't think they don't necessarily know that some of this stuff goes on, Gez. It suits them to have something else going on outside the Dome."

"Suits them?"

"Yeah, think about it. This Dome is one great big test lab. You need stuff to test against, right?"

Gerry shook his head, still unsure what to believe. He couldn't believe that the Family would deceive them that far. With the control over the population, they didn't need to. But then need and want weren't necessarily the same thing.

Gabe approached the train, pressed a button on the outside of the carriage, and the door slid back. Gabe stood aside with his arms open. "Welcome to Salvation Train Service," he said with a grin. "Please mind the step."

Petal took Gerry by the elbow and led him in. They took a seat, and Petal slid in next to him.

"Read up, code monkey," Petal said. "We got a lot of evil to dump." Petal sat next to Gerry on the plastic seat and looped her arm around his. "This is gonna be fun," she said with a wicked smile.

Gerry returned her smile, though his was pained and lopsided. Anxiety grew within him like hungry, urgent bacteria.

"What the hell have I got myself into?"

"The salvation business, man," Gabe said.

"The pay's crap, but the satisfaction is good for the soul," Petal said with a wink.

"Okay, let's do this. But once you're sorted, I want you guys to help me reach my family."

Petal and Gabe remained silent as the door to the train slid shut and the electric motors whined up to speed. They headed deeper into the disused tunnels. Gerry turned his head and watched the light of the platform shrink to the size of a pinhead before finally disappearing, taking his old life with it.

A new light shone in the far distance: a light beyond the city, into uncharted territory, into a land that no one he'd ever known had ventured since the rebuild. It was forbidden. The penalty was death—like almost every misdemeanour against the Family—and he, along with two people he'd known for just a few hours, were hurtling towards it in a train that should have been mothballed with all the others over fifty years ago.

There was a name for the place he was going: Purgatory. All his life he was told there was nothing out there. The Cataclysm had wiped out everything, and yet despite that, despite the evidence to the contrary, here he was rolling to a frightening new phase of his life with two anomalies, outliers, freaks.

When he saw his reflection in the window, he realised he looked just like them.

His new life was starting. A man reborn.

Chapter 5

The train came to a stop at a decrepit platform a few minutes later. Old posters peeled from tiled walls. Mould colonised the paper, creating a map of its own organic tracks. Dark shapes skittered along the platform in the angle where the wall met the floor. Rats. Living creatures. Something Gerry hadn't seen in City Earth. There were pets and animals, sure, but certainly not living, just constructs to make people feel comfortable. It worked, of course. Not that he knew any different. A cat running on a Cemprom chipset and AI logic was enough for most people, but Gerry could tell there was something missing there: a lack of a spark, real randomness. But that was to be expected. The degree of AI in those things was barely above children's toys. Still, most people were happy with them, happy to settle for a close approximation.

"What do they eat?" he asked.

"Sometimes people try to escape, find these old tunnels, and well... not many make it. Don't have a train like us, see," Petal said. "We're getting off here, Gez. Need to get you kitted out."

Petal and Gabriel alighted from the train and headed towards one of the mould-covered posters.

"Wait here a sec, Gez," Petal said, as she approached the wall with Gabe.

A simple hand gesture from her elicited a red LED beam from the wall. It scanned her eye, and the poster, attached to a door, opened. Petal waited for Gabriel to crawl up into the dark gap before turning back, beckoning to Gerry.

He barely squeezed his large frame into the tunnel. Only the sliding of Petal's and Gabriel's shoes against the stone surfaces gave him any sense of direction. For hundreds of metres he crawled on hands and knees, occasionally scraping the crown of his head against the rough, low surface.

"How long does this go on for?" He tried to hide the strain in his voice, but the tremble was still evident. His breath became shallow, the confines of the small space crushing down on his psyche, making his chest feel as if someone stood on it, squeezing the air from his lungs.

His elbows and knees burned as they rubbed against the concrete. All he wanted to do was stretch out, but the tunnel remained unforgiving.

"Breathe, Gez. We'll be out in a bit."

How long was a bit? Seconds? Minutes? Hours? It felt like he'd been stuck in there for years already. He focused on the rhythm of shuffles ahead of him, counted his movements, listened to his breathing. Anything to not think about the mass that surrounded him like a tomb.

Up ahead, the pitch-black void took on a slate grey aura, and as he neared, its luminosity increased until finally Gabe pushed open another door. Artificial sunlight flooded the tunnel, covering Gerry as if it were a cleansing shower of healing water. He scrambled faster, wanting to reach the light before it went out.

Stretching his cramped legs, Gerry breathed a deep sigh of relief, letting out all the pent-up, trapped anxiety. Resting his hands on his knees, he waited for his back muscles to relax. All around him, the light beamed down from a solid OLED panel in the low ceiling of the room. The room itself was nothing more than a concrete cupboard. A vertical tomb this time. At least he could actually stand here.

Petal tapped him on the shoulder. "Just through here."

Gabe took out his HackSlate, punched a series of finger gestures across its surface and waited. Two long seconds later, another door opened.

"I take it no one else knows this place is here?" Gerry asked as he followed Petal and Gabe into a larger room.

His answer came not from Gabe or Petal but from the unwelcome crackling of electricity from a stun-baton.

A black-masked figure shifted like a shadow and struck out with the baton, catching a bobbing Gabe on the shoulder. The force threw him back, knocking Petal to the ground and collapsing into Gerry's arms.

The shadow phased closer, and the baton arced through the air again. Gerry twitched away, closed his eyes, and involuntarily tensed up, fully expecting to feel that surge of power through his nervous system for the second time that day.

It didn't come.

All he heard was a low guttural choke and then the clatter as the baton crashed to the floor.

"Damned rat-bag. A breach? How the hell did she break our security?"

Petal stood wide-legged over the rumpled body of a woman in a black fabric suit. It no longer shifted in and out of the visual spectrum. It, like the woman wearing it, was no longer operational. Blood pooled from a twenty-millimetre hole created by a chromed spike extruding from the inside of Petal's right forearm. She lifted it into the air, flicked back her wrist, and the spike telescopically shot back within a hidden subdermal sheath. Very clever. It made Gerry wonder what other tricks Petal hid under her sleeves—literally.

"Who, or what, is that?" Gerry asked.

"Ninjas, man. This is gettin' serious."

"You okay, Gabe?"

The hacker rubbed his shoulder, squinted. "Been better."

"This ninja, who would have sent her, and why here?"

"We know why, man. That ain't the problem. It's by who that's the issue."

Gabe stepped over the corpse and motioned for Gerry to follow.

Racks standing over head height and extending five metres wide were filled with computers, cables, and more of that meshlike fibre-optic cabling. It looped from the top of the rack and ran across the ceiling and down the sides. Lights pulsed like fat pills through the cables as data flowed through the gas-filled tubes.

"Another secure network, I assume? Like your home?"

"Yeah, something like that, man."

"It's actually a Meshwork hub. The only one in City Earth, or I should say under it. No Family members can trace this. Like infiltrating from the inside. It's how we track the AIs and stuff. Anyway, let's see what the thief was after."

Petal withdrew a HackSlate from her leather coat's

breast pocket. "Crap a doodle-do. Seems your pals from Cemprom have been tracking you, Gez."

Gerry and Gabe huddled around Petal's HackSlate. It streamed video, presumably from a hidden camera in their home. So much for it being secure.

"That's Jasper!"

The white-haired man, dressed in a perfectly tailored suit, led a team of heavily armed security.

"Is this live?"

"Nah, about five minutes ago."

The video showed Jasper entering Gabe and Petal's home through the smouldering remains of the front door. The haze of smoke marred the high-definition video. Jasper and his team systematically tore through the place, ripping out wires, scanning each nook and cranny.

"What are they looking for?"

"Traffic. They must've bugged you or had at least some kind of surveillance to have found our place. It's secure as a gnat's chuff on a winter's day, but they ain't blind. They can see our mesh protection. I don't think this Jasper is the wet-behind-the-ears kid you think he is. That dude's got some serious game face. He knows what's going down."

Jasper followed two wiry security women into the kitchen and approached the dead body of Mike. He crouched and lifted what was left of Mike's head and stuck his fingers right into the eye socket, pulling out a wire. Taking a thinner slate, he attached the wire from Mike's head and plugged it in. After a few seconds, Jasper disconnected, stood, and nodded to his team.

One of the members carrying a smouldering large shoulder-mounted weapon stepped forward and doused the body with steaming liquid, turning Mike into nothing more than soggy pulp.

"Poor Mike... this is... just..."

"Work of the devil, man. Ya pal Jasper ain't no good. No good at all," Gabe said.

"What the hell does all this mean?"

"You know as much as we do," Petal said, closing the video and gesturing across the surface of her slate again. A string of numbers flowed down before coming to a stop. "Log files say the ninja didn't change a thing. She managed to get into our system, but didn't touch a damn thing."

"Maybe she was just doing some reconnaissance?" Gerry was clutching at straws and had no clue as to what was going on. Why would Jasper connect to Mike's... what exactly? His brain? Some kind of internal storage system? He'd known Mike since they were toddlers. He'd have known if he had any kind of cybernetic implants.

"You might be onto something there, Gez. I know one thing. She ain't working for Jasper or the Family. Look at this." Petal played another video. "This must have been just before we found her going by the time code."

Jasper, seemingly satisfied with his business with Mike, approached the secret door leading to the old escalator when he suddenly turned his head. Piercing screams sounded from outside the kitchen. The video switched to the camera in the living room. Jasper's entire security squad collapsed to the floor, simultaneously holding their ears. Their eyes distended, and veins popped from their foreheads. With a unified, horrific scream, the squad fled from the house.

Jasper ran into the shot, ran his hands through his

hair, and spun away from the scene. Clenching a fist, he screamed at the walls before chasing after his squad.

"Ninja here must've set off our local EMP. Wow, it actually worked. Though this tells us something about your pal Jasper," Petal said.

"It does?"

"Yeah, it tells us he ain't on any network. The boy's all flesh. No implants for him, otherwise he'd have been as fried as his little security detail there—unless he's got some kind of internal dampener…" Petal pursed her lips, thinking.

"So this woman was helping us?" Gerry said.

Gabe shook his head. "No. This is what they want. The Family. This Jasper's a fine actor—he knew what was gonna happen. With the EMP activated, our security's blasted to the great hard drive in the sky. Our Meshwork hub here and node up there are the only ways into City Earth's wider network. It's how we make our money, ya see. We use our tech to track these AIs that are trying to do bad stuff, and we exorcise 'em. Only now, it seems we've been found out, and someone is using our gear to crack the network."

"Damn it. You're right, Gabe." Petal frantically gestured across her HackSlate, shaking her head. "That other demon AI's all over the place, piggybacking on our Meshwork to attack City Earth's defences, which, now you and your pal Mike are out of the game, are severely weakened."

"But Jasper is from the Family," Gerry said. "Why would he sabotage the very city that belongs to him and his kind? It doesn't make any sense. The guy is on the inside. If he wanted to get to Kuznetski, he'd just do it himself or use one of his relations. They rule this place. They don't need to resort to all this nonsense just to get rid of the president."

Gabe smiled. "So what does that tell ya, man?"

Gerry tried to think. As expected, his reliance on Mags, his AIA, had slowed his analytical thinking. He was tired, weak, and just couldn't think. "I don't know!" He kicked out at the woman on the floor. "This ain't me—I don't know all this stuff. I'm just a regular guy who's been screwed over." He wanted to explode. The frustration built in his head so that he thought he'd completely lose the plot, but then, like a supernova, the answer came to him.

"Jasper isn't from the Family! Holy crap. He's the insider... the hacker. He's the swine that put the demon AI into Mike... and me. He must have been working with her." Gerry nudged the woman again with a toe, fully expecting her to jump at the revelation.

"I think ya right, man. It's logical. Enna could probably shed some light on this."

"Enna?"

"Someone who hires us," Petal said. "She gives us contracts, deals in information. She'll pay big for this." Her toothy grin was back, not from the situation but from the results of a NanoStem injection. The syringe stuck out of a raised vein on her forearm.

"Don't look so freaked out, Gez. Think of this as medicine, yeah? I need it to help hold all this stuff in... I've a weak immune system; hence why we should get you geared up pronto. Talking of which, Gez, come here."

Gerry stepped towards Petal, and that's all he remembered.

***

A jabbing pain in his neck woke Gerry up. Touching it, he felt something cold and hard. Something made from metal. "What the hell?"

"It's just a connection port, man," Gabe said. "Ya'll need it outside of the City. We had to put ya under. It can be messy."

Gabriel was right. Next to Gerry's foot lay a crimson pool. When he inspected his hand, spots of blood covered his fingertips. "It hurts like hell. Was this entirely necessary?" Gerry leant over and waited for a wave of nausea to pass. Neck ports weren't unheard of. City Earth citizens had them up to a few years ago when they were outlawed due to the new all-encompassing wireless network.

Petal slapped him on the butt. "We've got work to do."

Gerry sat back down on the plastic seat inside the train carriage and admired his new leather duster jacket and strong boots. The gun belt made carrying the revolver easier.

He was concerned about the numbness in his neck. Gabe gave him a shot of NanoStem to ease the pain, and he could understand Petal's previous expression. It was delicious. Like being carried on wings of air. It felt almost as if he were sleepwalking with all his faculties turned up to max. It even felt like he had use of Mags again. Thoughts processed so quickly he couldn't get a handle on them. Knew that eventually all that computation, all that analysis of the day's events would deliver a result and unravel the mystery of who Jasper was, or working for, and who was behind the malicious AI apparently gunning for Miralam Kuznetski.

"Okay, Gez," Petal said. "I want you to access your dermal implant and enter this code: oh-forty-seven-hash-three-hash-one-nine-fifty-eight-colon-six. That'll connect you to our short-range, virtual private network. Our VPN. Once the NanoStem wears off and you can fully interact with your neck port, we'll be able to communicate securely and send data to each other. Where we're going, we're gonna need it: it's a dangerous place out there in… the abandoned lands."

"Sure. No problem. I got it." Without thinking he did as he was told, and he felt a slight buzz of electricity in his dermal implant.

Petal was saying something again. Her voice lilted and floated as if it were some far-off song from an audio system. He knew what she was saying was important and useful, but he just let the words flow through his brain, socket themselves into places that he'd recover later. For now, he was just pleased to be numb—to let the grief and heartache melt away like ice on a summer's day.

His eyelids grew too heavy to resist. Leaning back, he gave in to the drugs and conjured memories of his two girls: they grew faint and indistinct, and the last thought he had before sleeping was that he couldn't remember exactly what they looked like.

Chapter 6

The clacking and whirring of the train penetrated Gerry's subconscious. The depth of his sleep became thin, like NanoSheets: parts of the real world transforming the cadre of diaphanous thoughts that ran through his mind.

The steady rhythm from outside melded with his frantic cogitations until, within his mind, all he saw was a stream of code. At first he couldn't make sense of the programmes—being made up with the symbols and characters from the old C language—but then, like a student of foreign languages, who, being thrown into the deep end with fluent speakers, soon started to understand: rhythms, grammar, syntax, logic, loops, statements, call-backs, variables, constants, objects… so much data—so much possibility.

The train screeched to a halt.

Gerry snapped his eyes open with a start, sucked in a breath, and gripped the handrail as if he were falling off a cliff.

Ahead of him bright light reduced his pupils to dust specks. The aurora of white light encompassed everything, so that for a minute, Gerry thought he was dead.

No one spoke. All around him, more blinding light… but there, in front of him in the next row, a head… dread-locks.

"Gabriel. Is that you?" His voice felt small, shaky, like a boy's.

The head turned.

Gabe's voice was hushed, filled with tension. "Quiet, Gez, we're approaching the toll. Let us handle this. You stay where you are, okay?"

A hand, cool and clammy, circled his forearm. Her grip delicate, like his grandmother's on her deathbed. The image struck Gerry like a bullet, and it was all he could do to choke down the welling up of emotion. A simple touch shouldn't be able to bring so much pain. He thought of his grandmother in her hospice: withered and grey. Her skin gone translucent so that her slow veins showed through like blue string. He, his wife, and his father sat around her—waiting. Her touch was the last thing she gave him.

A tear fell down Gerry's cheek. It reached halfway before another soft, caring hand wiped it away.

Petal slipped across the plastic seat until her warmth radiated into his leg and ribs.

"It's okay, Gerry. I understand. You get used to it. You'll forget. Well, in my case the memories faded for other reasons. S'all part of the job. You'll get through it, Gez. I promise."

The train came to a full stop. Its motors whined down, and the doors slid open with a whoosh of air.

Petal gave his arm a quick squeeze before standing up. "We'll be right back. Let us scope it out first. We ain't in Paradise anymore. They'll 'love' the likes of you. All fresh and innocent."

"Who will?"

Petal gave him a quirky, side-lilting smile and flipped over her mirrored lenses on her goggles. "The natives... let's just say they're a little eager."

At her wild expression and hint of what might be out there, Gerry pulled the gun from the bag and took comfort from its entirely mechanical coldness.

"That's m'boy. You shoot like hell if anything... weird comes your way, you hear?"

"Wait, what? Weird? Weird how?"

"You'll know. Sit tight, precious."

Petal turned and joined Gabriel on the grey stone platform outside of the train. It was no more than a few metres wide, and the stained, tiled wall curved upwards, creating an archway over the train. Gerry admired the organic nature of it: real materials, real handwork. He felt its gravity and presence. Qualities so often missing in nanotube-based materials and holo-projections. Beyond the platform, the train tunnel opened to a cloudless grey-blue sky. Red dust rose and spun into miniature twisters from the parched, bare ground. On the horizon, low and blocky, a series of buildings gathered together like a pack of sleeping dogs.

So this is the scorched earth... the results of the Cataclysm, Gerry thought as he pondered the nature of those buildings. Clearly not everything had been destroyed.

The wind picked up, changed direction, and blew his way.

He breathed in the scent: it smelled wet and heavy with promises, adventure, and danger—of times past, times before the Cataclysm. Nothing survived, they said. All was lost. Now, he knew different. Something did… out there in the dust another living thing existed. He tapped his foot eagerly as he gripped his gun. Gerry was never a patient man. The waiting pulled at him with the weight of gravity, of the tides, of that terrible yearning that boiled within him.

A deep breath and he calmed his nerves.

Petal and Gabriel looked back at him, faces straight, and then they turned a corner out of sight.

***

How long should he have waited? Gabe and Petal didn't say, but they hadn't returned in what must have been ten minutes. Or was it ten hours? While he waited, Gerry devoured the first three chapters of the *Hacking With Helix* book like a child discovering ice cream for the first time.

Imprinted on his mind, like maps, were exploit algorithms, defence mechanisms, early warning systems, and attack ideologies. For the first time in his life he felt like it was actually him who was capable of doing this stuff and not his AIA.

A thrill of excitement ran through him as he pictured himself exorcising demonic AIs like Gabe. The potential and the power—via his own mind and not through a preprogrammed device—made him feel more alive than he could remember. But it didn't last.

A scream, certainly from Petal, erupted from outside and echoed down the tunnel.

Grabbing the bag and gripping the gun, Gerry ignored their advice and bolted out of the carriage onto the platform. He sprinted the hundred-or-so metres to the exit and spun left.

Gabriel lay at an awkward angle: bent over himself at the foot of a four-metre-high tower. It was barely wide enough to house two people. It looked like a stack of kids' grey building blocks. A shadow moved behind a small glass window at head height.

Petal stood to the side of the tower. She, too, was bent over, but still on her feet. Blood oozed from her mouth into a dark pool on the dusty earth.

Gerry rushed over.

Petal turned. "Go back!"

"What's happened?" Gerry asked, wondering if Gabe was dead.

Before Petal could respond, a door in the side of the tower creaked open, and a round metal barrel extended from the gloom. Petal grabbed at Gerry's shirt and pulled him aside as a thunderous explosion erupted from the gun. He'd never heard such a deep, powerful explosion before. It made his guts squirm.

He fell to the floor, scrabbling in the sickly pool of blood as Petal tried to pull him away from the corner of the tower. A low, heavy voice called out in frustration from within the tower. "You burnt-out, cheap hacking swines!"

The metal door flung open and clanged against the tower. Two heavy footsteps thudded into the dirt, and when Gerry looked up, a man wearing thick, black coveralls and wielding a large, long-barrelled gun blotted out the light. He was as wide as two men side by side. Gerry couldn't make out his features in the silhouette but felt the hatred emanating from him.

The man pointed the barrel at Gerry, who continued to scrabble on his back like a stuck beetle.

"This a new friend, huh, Petal? Not anymore…"

As the man moved his finger over the trigger, Petal spun round. The chromed spike as long as her arm extended from her palm with a snap. She drove it with all the weight of her body into the man's ribs, sending the barrel into the air as he sent another booming shot into the empty sky. He howled as he spun round, dragging Petal with him.

"Gez! Help. Shoot him!"

The gun! Where was his gun? He must have dropped it as he fell. While the man was crushing Petal against the tower and screaming in pain, Gerry frantically searched the ground on all fours for the gun. Another metallic crash and the man continued to smash Petal up against the tower. Each impact brought a grunt of anguish from the pair of them as Petal's spike remained in his ribs.

Touching the coldness of the gun's handle, Gerry snatched it up. His hand wobbled as he took aim. The first shot went wide, but the second caught his knee, sending the man to the ground, taking Petal with him. He hit the ground hard, crushing Petal beneath his weight.

She tried to pull her arm free, screaming as his bulk continued to crush her small, fragile body.

Petal managed to gasp a single word between snatched breaths. "Help—"

Gerry rushed over, tried to force the man over, but he weighed considerably more than a normal man should. Petal's head hit the dirt. The lenses of her goggles turned red, and for a split second, she looked like a damaged, discarded doll—still and broken.

Anger welled up inside his guts like boiling water. His vision narrowed until all he could see was the man's massive head. He, too, wore goggles, but they were covered in sand and dust. He sported a pair of sick-looking scars across his right cheek, and numerous jack ports punctured his neck.

Moving his gun against the man's head, Gerry closed his eyes and fired a single bullet. His shaking hand and struggling target conspired to send his bullet wide. The shot ricocheted off the tower with a spark.

The man thrust out a hand and grabbed Gerry by the leg. His grip felt like it would snap his bone. Panicked, Gerry raised the gun again and, despite his tremble, managed to aim the gun and fire accurately.

The gore of the man's skull and brain muffled the shot.

The tower, once dull and grey, now featured a red and bone-coloured paint job.

With a lunatic's strength and the monsoon of adrenaline that threatened to drown him, he finally managed to push to one side the dead piece of meat. He pulled Petal out from under him, and her long, thin conelike weapon slipped out of his rib cage with a sucking noise.

Her once pale face was now decorated with an ugly purple-black bruise. Her lip puffed twice its regular size and was split down the middle. She coughed, and Gerry's relief threatened to bring him to the ground. "You're alive! Petal, are you okay?"

She nodded slowly and rubbed at her chest.

Gabriel moaned and turned his head to Gerry. He

looked worse than Petal. His skin was almost as grey as the tower. A wire from his neck trailed across the ground to a small rusted box attached to the outside of the tower.

"Gabe! You okay?"

He nodded his head slowly. His eyes squeezed tightly closed. Petal reached up and gripped Gerry's hand to get his attention. "You gotta stop the alarm. Within minutes every City Earth border goon will be on us like flies on crap." She frantically pointed to the open door to the tower.

Inside, a single console with a holographic projector showed a large circle surrounded by a concentric ring. Along this ring, there were at least fifty, maybe more, small squares. Gerry guessed these were the towers. The circle, he assumed, was probably City Earth.

There were no obvious ways of manipulating or connecting to the console.

One of the squares began to flash, and outside, a siren began to tear through the atmosphere.

"I can't stop it!" Gerry searched the console and all round the small room. It was empty: just a chair and the damned projection of the map.

He stuck his head outside, looking at Petal and Gabriel, who were helping each other up. Then Gerry caught on: the wire coming from Gabe's neck into the box.

"Gabe, how do I connect? With that box?"

Gabriel smiled and shook his head. "You gotta go in deeper. Like the guard here…" Gabriel kicked at the man's head until it rolled over, facing Gerry. His goggles were ripped to shreds from the gun blast. Inside one eye socket something glinted—something metallic.

"Ever hacked a dead man?" Gabe said.

Chapter 7

Gerry helped Gabriel to his feet and looked away as the older man removed the jack plug from his neck. Despite his own newly fitted ports, he still couldn't get used to the idea of plugging hardware into one's self. It wasn't natural.

"You'll get used to it eventually, man," Gabriel said as he let the cable drop to the dusty ground.

"It's part of you now, part of your job," Petal said.

"Job? I didn't ask for this." Gerry slumped against the tower and eased the pain in his neck. His whole body felt like taut rope. "What do you need me to do?"

Gabriel twisted his neck and stretched his arms. He looked rough: heavy bags under his eyes and a network of bloodshot veins infiltrating his corneas. Gabe kicked at the massive corpse. "This guard right 'ere is usually accommodating, but he got greedy, wanted more than we could afford. That box over there that I was connected to—that's a donation box. It took all my bins and refused to let us through. Something's changed. I need you to get inside his head, crack his AIA, switch off the alarm, and see what's going on. And you've probably got about five minutes to do it before we're executed by his pals."

"He's dead. See—no brains left. What do you expect me to find?"

Petal's face lit up with a wicked grin.

"What?" Gerry asked as Gabe joined Petal in their secret glee. It felt like he was back at first school. A green, know-nothing kid.

"You really don't know? Oh, that's real precious. The Family have you lot completely duped."

Gerry was losing his patience and irritation started to prickle at his skin. It was that or the heat. Now that he was out of the protection of City Earth's dome and subsequent controlled microclimate, the natural rays of the sun were beginning to burn a little on his skin. It wasn't entirely unpleasant, but it wasn't helping him keep his cool.

Petal's smile dropped, and she looked to the ground. "Sorry, Gez. Let me explain." She bent down next to the corpse. She took a leather glove from a pocket on her combat trousers and put it on before reaching into the cavity of what was left of the guard's head. The brain mulch squelched as she searched for something.

"See this here? You can plug directly into it and get into his AIA. It's how he operated the terminal."

"I'm sorry, I don't understand. If you know all this, why are you asking me to do it? And that's disgusting, not to mention disrespectful."

"He tried to kill us. What d'ya expect? A perfect burial?" Gabe said.

"You're a priest. Shouldn't you be like, you know…"

"I believe in no god, Gez. I'm a different kind of priest, and you'll learn all this soon enough. Look, Petal's storage is full to bursting. If she tries anything, all hell will break loose. And I'm not talking biblical hell here, not that you'd know about any of that. The Family have seen to that, haven't they? Besides, this… thing ain't no human. How many people do you know have port leads in their spinal column?"

That confused feeling washed over Gerry again. It was like they were all talking a different language. Finally losing his temper, he grabbed Gabriel by the lapels of his longer duster jacket. "Just explain why it's me that has to do this. And tell me how. I don't understand anything you're saying. And what the hell is it if it's not a person?"

"We call 'em 'NearlyMen'. They're a new design. Part of the Family's security force for City Earth."

"There's no one left to get into the City since the Cataclysm, surely?"

"Who said they're only trying to keep people out? Why do you think we were paying a bribe? Only way out to the abandoned lands is through this here gate system. Look, we're running out of time. We're being patient because this is your first time, but jack in and get on with it. Figure it out while you're inside."

Petal grabbed a lead from her backpack. She plugged one end into the gore-covered port inside the NearlyMan and the other into the jack socket in Gerry's neck.

His natural reaction was to jerk away, but Gabriel held him tight and whispered into his ear. "Use your algorithm skills to sniff out the security protocol, Gez. When inside, disable the alarm and open the gate. You'll see inside clearly enough. These NearlyMen don't have much else going on in there."

Before he could speak, his brain pulsed like it was trying

to escape his skull from the inside. A burning white pain shot through his eye nerves, and he twitched uncontrollably as he connected with the NearlyMan's AIA.

Gerry didn't see it as much as he felt it. A black entity of sorts hovering in the corner of an empty room. He mentally approached it and thought of a way to communicate with it. Outside of his mind, everything had dulled to a low hum. Even the heat on his skin from the sun was now just a fading memory. It was just him and the intelligent program.

In a sweet female voice, it spoke to Gerry. "You've been a naughty boy. Daddy will not be happy."

Gerry ignored it and continued to probe for a way past its security system. Each check, each test was rebuffed with error code #2501: insufficient talent.

It was mocking him.

Reaching out his mind and thinking back to the code samples he remembered from the exploits book, he pictured a complicated algorithm and sent it towards the security module. He felt his heartbeat increase. The AIA processed his thoughts as though they were executable code. It took Gerry's breath away. He'd never felt anything so… immediate.

Excited, he threw more code at it. Unburdened by having to type or speak code and waiting for it to compile like his daily work back at Cemprom, he just thought his code and there it was, unfolding, executing, running.

"You know, little boy, I'm starting to like you," the AIA said.

It was becoming overwhelmed with Gerry's code viruses. He felt the first layer of security break down, and he extended his thoughts further into the darkened room: a representation of the NearlyMan's storage drive. The AIA recognised Gerry as an owner of the system, and he was free to explore its contents as if he were the guard.

The first thing he did was switch the flag on the AIA's speech file to Off. That was trivial. Next up was the alarm system. Luckily, it was like Gabe had said. There was very little in this system. Apart from the AIA's protected files and the guard's personality profile and behaviour instructions, there were just two areas left: the alarm protocols and one named Personal.

Intrigued, Gerry opened the latter section. Inside, a gallery of images floated up in his mind. There were thousands of the same two scenes from the limited view from the tower. Some looking towards City Earth, others looking away. Of those looking away, Gerry noticed specks of dark colour on the horizon. He flicked through them in time order, the specks growing larger, until the later images showed what looked... no, couldn't be... a group of women and men dressed in what looked like furs and leathers. Some sported riflelike weapons, while others had wires, antennae, and dish shaped objects mounted upon their person.

People.

Other people from the abandoned lands.

Unbelievable. But there it was, right there in the AIA. Hard proof. This meant the Family had lied. Growing up, Gerry was taught that all the survivors from the Cataclysm—which was never fully explained—were in City Earth and there was no one left outside.

What else was a lie?

Gerry casually switched off the alarm system, exited from the AIA, and pulled the plug from his neck. He looked at Petal and Gabe, who in turn looked at him like feverish cats.

"They lied," Gerry said before slumping to the ground, clutching his head as a bolt ripped through his brain.

Chapter 8

Petal shook his arm. "You okay, Gez?"

He blinked, saw her face hovering over his, blotting out the sun. Her goggles were clear. Her eyes were bright violet this time. They shimmered like the surface of a lake. Before he could speak, her goggles turned opaque again, cutting him off from those amazing colours.

"We don't have much time," she said with a whisper.

Her skin seemed paler than usual. Her hand felt clammy against his skin.

He wanted to ask what would happen if she could no longer hold the demons, but the pained expression on her face told him it wasn't going to be anything good.

"It's done," he finally said. "I managed to switch off the alarm system. But I—"

"What is it?" Gabe said. He lifted Gerry to his feet and held him by his shoulders. He peered directly into Gerry's eyes with fervour.

"People. I saw pictures of… other people."

"Yeah, about them." Gabe rubbed his face. "Not everything the Family has told you is true. Well, hardly anything at all, as it happens. There's a few survivors out here. Ya gonna meet some real soon. 'Specially now you handled the alarm system. I'm impressed, man. That was slick. Ya picking this up quickly."

"Who are we going to see?" Gerry asked.

"Some old buddies of a sort. Reload your gun. Ya know, just in case."

Petal took a piece of brain fragment from the corpse and tossed it against the filament fence. It just hit the wires and fell to the ground.

"It's all safe. We need to get going. I don't think I've got much time."

Gerry reloaded his gun from the ammo pack in his bag. As they moved towards the fence, he bent and picked up the heavy shotgun from the guard and placed it in his bag. He wasn't sure whether it would be any use without more shells, and he had little time to search for them, but it couldn't hurt to take it with them just in case.

Gabriel bent over, stepped through the gap in the wire fence, and Gerry and Petal followed. Up ahead on the horizon a rust-red cloud billowed up. A low growling noise rumbled on the wind.

Gerry turned to Petal, who was now moving much slower, wincing at each step. "That your friends?" He pointed to the scenes of movement ahead.

Petal nodded. "Kinda." She extended the chromed spike from her palm and gritted her teeth. "Just watch your back, Gez. These aren't the same as the people back in City Earth."

"Got it."

"Seriously," Petal said. "Out here things ain't so polite. You ain't got security looking out for you either. It's like the Wild West, Gez."

Gabe continued to walk onwards, setting a quick pace. They travelled for fifteen minutes until the cloud was no more than a few hundred metres away. The small, squat buildings Gerry saw before now held more detail.

Plates of metal, wood, and wire mesh covered their surface. Spikes the size of a man extended out from their perimeter. A fence stretched for half a kilometre either side of this makeshift town. A tall gate sat in the middle— partially open.

From the gap, a series of vehicles, bikes, trikes, and large-wheeled buggies streamed out. Their drivers wore little apart from partial furs and goggles.

Gerry swallowed, wanting to wash it down with the water Gabe had brought, but realised he'd only been out of the Dome for a short while and the others showed no sign of needing refreshment. He didn't want to look so weak so soon.

The sun bore down on him, seemingly cooking his skin to a crisp. How Gabriel could suffer wearing his leather duster coat, Gerry had no idea. He'd taken off his own coat as soon as they got through the fence and rolled his sleeves up to his shoulders, yet he was still sweating as if in a sauna.

"Hot for spring," Gerry said.

"It ain't usual," Petal said. "Make the most of it. Usually it's just cold and dry."

Petal held up her hand to shield the light from her goggles and stared out at the oncoming cavalcade.

He didn't like the silence from Gabe or Petal. Both just stared right ahead, watching the group of survivors get closer. Gerry wondered what to call them. Were they survivors? Was their little town a country or city of its own? Who ruled over it? How did they grow food? Myriad questions flowed through his mind as he attempted to beat down the nerves that grew more strained as they drew ever closer. He asked the questions to Petal, wanting to break the tense silence that had built up.

Petal turned to Gerry. "They call themselves Bachians. Bachia was a province in this area many decades ago. They're small provincials with smaller minds."

"You said they were your buddies?"

"Hah, that was Gabe. He was being sarcastic. Our last interaction with them wasn't so good. As for food, it's like most of us out here: soy protein and occasionally corn. Few crops grow, or survive, for long in the poisoned soil. It's getting better, though. The soy filters out a lot of the heavy metals and radiation. There's all kinds of recipes now."

"Sounds, erm… nice."

"It's shit for the most part," Petal said. "Sometimes we get lucky and find some of the freeze-dried ration packs on our travels. Usually we just steal food from the Dome, as do the Bachians."

Gerry raised an eyebrow, questioning.

"Yeah, that's where they get a lot of their resources. Tunnels, Gez. And like I said before, the Family tolerate them to a degree."

Gerry wanted to probe her for more information, but she cut off as they came closer. Finally, she said, "We'll need their help. Old Grey's in their possession."

"Old Grey?"

Petal nodded, displaying her lupine smile. "You'll fill your pants when you get a load of Old Grey. She's been around longer than all of us. Well, apart from Gabe, that is. Never met anyone or anything older than him." She cackled as Gabe turned his head at the sound of her voice.

"So who is this Old Grey? A survivor from before the Cataclysm?"

"Kinda. It's a computer. An ancient AI-based server with a hard-on for malicious code. It's where I unload my storage. She's super rare. These Bachians worship her like a god."

Gerry thought of the possibilities: if this computer was as old as Petal said, it would have petabytes of information about the world before the Cataclysm, before the Family and the building of City Earth. "Can you get access to its data storage?"

"Haha, you're a funny guy, Gez. I admire your ambition. Nah, Old Grey is tight as a gnat's ass. Access to her is tightly controlled."

"What about remote access?"

Petal stopped, pulling at Gerry's elbow. "Why're you so interested?"

"I want the truth. What you and Gabe have highlighted for me recently is just how much bullshit we've been fed by the Family. Despite City Earth supposedly being a utopia, it seems someone is desperate to bring it down. I'd like to know why." If he could find out what happened, maybe he could understand the Family. Understand their control. At the heart of that was another central question that he often wondered about. Who was he, really?

"Well, I'm all for shady shenanigans, but if you're planning anything, wait until I've downloaded all this crap. I don't want to be cut off mid-dump."

"Eloquent."

"I mean it, Gez. I get you're angry and want answers, but be patient, yeah?"

"Sure. I'm sorry. This is all new to me. I'm just trying to find my bearings."

"Come on. Let's go meet some Bachians. And a dear old enemy. You think your mind is blown now, wait till you meet Bilanko. She's the guardian of Old Grey. Freaks me out every time we have to meet her. Assuming she's still there."

"Why's that such a problem? Move around much, does she?"

"Yup. Never in the same place for more than a few days. Always seeking information, bartering, dealing, analysing."

The sound of their engines grew above Petal's voice. Vibrations from their movement juddered through the ground and up into Gerry's legs. How could they stand the noise and the dust? It was a far cry from the clean, quiet, electric vehicles back home. And yet, despite that, there was something alluring about the smoke-belching, loud, rough machines. It was a display of power that you just don't get with the cold efficiency of electric.

"How are they fuelling the engines?" Gerry asked.

"H-core, Gez. Altered hydrogen fuel cells taken from the electric vehicles that got screwed up in the EMP. That and a highly unstable mix of fermented soy oil. Not many vehicles around anymore, at least not ones that are serviceable. Too many dead electronics, you see. What's left are make-dos like the Bachia stuff here. Further afield I saw a few aircraft and trucks. Most of them were fixed and repaired, running off hydrogen fuel. The Bachian's have got a small refinery they use to get hydrogen from rain."

"What rain?" Gerry asked, surveying the dry, cracked earth for as far as he could see. It clearly hadn't rained in some time.

"Exactly," Petal said. "Hence why this lot don't travel very far, and why in general there's so few vehicles. Commodities, Gez, they are rare. Or at least the ones that can't be stolen from the Family."

"So how they get water?"

"There's a few wells. Most settlements are usually around them. It's like the old days back in Africa. We go where the water is—or where we're not likely to get killed. They purify it here, too. Carbon filters and a natural trap with soy plants to take out the dangerous stuff."

Gerry could already feel his throat getting dry.

The group of vehicles, ten of them in total, pulled up a few feet from Gabriel, who was now some ten metres or so ahead of Gerry and Petal. Gerry wanted to speed up and make ground, but Petal was slowing down, stumbling, and he couldn't leave her behind. Gabe had seemingly trusted Gerry to look after her as he met with the group first.

A wiry, bald man hopped out of the cage that surrounded his buggy. His ragged and dusty leather jerkin flapped in the wind. He wiped the red dirt from his goggles and grinned as he stretched out a hand to Gabriel.

Gabe slapped it away with his left hand and punched the man in the face, splitting his nose with a vicious right jab.

A whoop of cheers and laughter erupted from the group.

Gerry and Petal caught up with Gabe and stood by his

side as he spoke to the group.

"I've got two thousand bins for the first person to give me their vehicle and the address of Bilanko Barnabas."

The goggled heads turned to each other while the man on the ground rolled over onto his back with a grimace. He spat out a tooth and a gob of blood before speaking. "Gabriel, old pal, old chum, why didn't you just say that's what you wanted? I'd have been more than willing to—"

Gabriel kicked the man in the ribs. A loud crack sounded, and the man yelped.

Reaching out, Gerry grabbed Gabriel by the shoulder. "Gabe, what's going on?"

"It's okay, now, man. I've got this."

"Don't interfere, Gez," Petal said. "There's bad blood here."

"Well? I'm waiting," Gabe said to the gang. "Either you take my generous offer or Spitty here ceases to be one of your number."

None of the group spoke. Some looked away while others looked at each other, confused.

There was movement from the back of the pack. A woman in tall boots and a fur skirt sauntered to the front between the vehicles. She carried a blade as long as her leg in her gloved right hand. A chain mail guard covered her shoulder and upper arm.

"Two thou' you say?" She flicked her short-cropped dark hair from her face, exposing almond-shaped brown eyes, which narrowed as she examined Gabe. Her hips pushed out in a provocative stance. "That all you got, Mr Techxorcist Man?"

"Hmm. Maybe for you, I've got a little something

extra—if you can get me to Bilanko right away without any pissing about."

"Aye. I can do that. Fastest trike this side of the Sludge. Show me your goods first, ol' man."

"What's ya name?"

"What the hell is it to you?"

"I like to know who I'm dealing with, is all."

She flicked her hair and flared her nostrils. "Cheska."

"Okay, Cheska." Gabe reached into the interior pocket of his jacket and pulled out a ten-centimetre-long Digi-Card with three small holes in a triangle formation at one edge.

"This card is loaded with three thousand bins. It's yours if we move right now. If not, ya gonna have to find this kinda cash elsewhere."

Gabe stared her down. She stepped casually from one foot to the other, weighing up her decision. While she was deciding, the man crawling on the ground holding his ribs moaned as Gabe prodded him with a boot.

Gerry turned to Petal and whispered, "What's the deal with that guy?"

Petal cupped her hand around his ear and whispered in turn. "Last time we were here, he tried to catch Gabe in a viral net."

"What does that do?" Gerry asked.

"Uploads malicious code direct to the cortex interface via the Meshwork. It'd put Gabe out of action for good. Look, being a Techxorcist is a precious commodity around these parts, and some nefarious hackers would rather there weren't one for hire. You're gonna need to learn to use that gun and protect yourself. This is the Wild West, Doc."

"You're a weird one, you know that?" Gerry said, smiling in spite of himself.

There was something about her, something fragile, wise. In some situations she reminded him of his eldest daughter, or his wife when he first met her. He pushed the thought away, not wanting to go there just yet. It was too raw. The tension was high enough already without him reminiscing.

Everyone waited in silence for the sword-woman to make up her mind.

She looked down at the writhing man. His skin was caked with red-brown dust. With a single stab, she drove the sword through his neck, slicing his carotid artery. Blood spurted a few feet in the air and covered her chest and shoulders. She turned to the stunned onlookers. "This is my operation now, you understand?"

To a woman and man, they nodded.

"Good," she said with a smirk. "I hated that piece of filth anyway, with his greasy little grabby hands and bent cock. You've done me a bit of a favour there, ol' man. You lot, come with me. You've got some cash to deliver, and I know where Bilanko's holing up. I'll warn you now. She ain't in no good mood. Damned drones been attacking all weekend long."

"Drones?" Gerry asked.

Cheska stepped to the side of Gabe and regarded Gerry with a 'who the hell are you' look.

"Got yourselves a new baby?"

"Mind your own damned business," Petal replied as she stepped forward, shoulders wide, legs planted.

Cheska laughed, turned her back, and beckoned them

to follow.

Petal turned to Gerry.

"City Earth occasionally sends out UAV drones to keep places like these under control. Like flocks of birds, but with hi-res cameras, integrated VPNs, and weaponry."

"What kind of weaponry?" Gerry scanned the dark skyline, expecting to see dark assassins flitting between the clouds.

"Lasers, particle beams, graphene-tipped ammunition... there's a bunch of different models."

Gerry shook his head. "Great. This place just gets better and better."

Gabe sat with Cheska in her vehicle. He turned to regard Petal. "Okay to drive you and Gez?"

"Sure," she said, grabbing Gerry's hand and pulling him to the now-vacant buggy.

Gerry hopped in and sat next to Petal as she took the wheel and stomped the throttle. The vehicle lurched forward with a roar of internal combustion, sending a plume of red dust in its wake. Gerry whooped and laughed at the madness of the situation. He felt free and alive, and for a brief moment he forgot who he was. But with all things that are forgotten, the memories have a habit of coming back.

His family, his life, his job—everything gone. But for that short moment it didn't matter.

The journey to the ramshackle town lasted just a few minutes as they powered on through the scrap metal gates. Following the lead of the woman, Petal pulled the buggy up at a slightly less battered building with a sign on the front: The Spider's Byte.

The leader of the gang jumped off her trike and strode towards the door. Gabe followed.

She whispered something, and Gabe passed her the card.

"Okay, suckers, Bilanko's in the back room. Good luck. I hope you come out alive. Mama always needs more bins." She winked at Gabe and headed off.

Gabe looked at Gerry. "Arm up, man. This place is volatile."

***

The bar's palpable darkness shrouded the three of them as they entered the building. The bright, dry atmosphere of the desertlike exterior seemed so far away now, as if in another dimension altogether. Gerry didn't know what the rules were here. Didn't know if physics were the same. What was the right etiquette? A feeling of being on that razor's edge of doing or saying something extremely dumb overwhelmed him entirely.

"What are we looking for, exactly?" Gerry said to Gabe, trying to calm his nerves.

"Bilanko, of course. You don't listen very well, do ya, man?"

"I know that. I mean, what or who is she? I can't see anything in here."

"Just chill ya bones, man. Take it easy and follow my lead."

To see Gabe and Petal shrink into themselves, become as non-threatening as possible, wasn't a sign that this place was a safe haven filled with people full of bon vivant and good intentions.

Beady, glowing eyes emerged from the gloom and struck Gerry in a series of non-blinking stares. The people to whom these augmented eyes belonged stayed deep in the shadows of their upholstered cubicles. Shot glasses of neon blue liquids littered their round metal tables.

Wheeze, clank, wheeze, clank.

The sound of a hundred shadowy patrons shooting their drinks and slamming the glasses to the table in unison created a kind of death march. Not one voice. Not one greeting. Even the bartender stood motionless with a filthy rag in one hand and a curved dagger in the other— laid casually on the rusted metal bar top as if to say, 'Here's my knife. It's in its happy place right now, but it won't hesitate to cut you.'

Gerry felt around his belt and found the comforting cold steel of his revolver. How quickly he'd grown to rely on it. Looking at these augments, he wondered whether he'd even be able to fire off a single round before they would jump and slice him. Who knew what other modifications these people had? Were they even people? It was hard to tell when all you could see were gloved hands gripping shot glasses and glowing amber and red eyes.

Below the bar floor a deep bass wave rumbled. It continued to build until it formed a pulsating rhythm right up into Gerry's guts. It gathered speed, beating quicker and quicker. His own heart's racing beat had now been outpaced, and then, to accompany the bass line, a synth wave wailed through the tense atmosphere.

Then the pounding of drums.

And just like that, the people were smiling, nodding

their heads to the rhythm, shooting their shots, surrounding the bar, and ordering more of whatever it was they were drinking.

Gerry let go of his gun, dropped his shoulders, and breathed out the tension. They weren't so important after all. Gabe and Petal led him through the throng of animated revellers.

The dancing crowd were dressed mostly in a matching uniform of sorts: black leather jackets, jeans, biker boots. Real old fashioned, like those his parents wore before all the new synthetic materials replaced denim and cotton. Many of them wore their hair like Petal's: bright pinks, greens, blues. A range of Mohicans, spikes and straggly mop-tops.

A group of eight women wearing tight, reflective trousers and pin-sharp stiletto boots stood by the cubicles and booths, assessing, recording, observing. Gerry recognised the serious and deadly body language of security. Though he saw no visible weapons, he was in no doubt they would be more than capable of handling themselves.

One in particular had eyeballed him as soon as the party got started. Her blazing white eyes reflected off her chromed headpiece. She looked like a piece of modern art, a sculpture. Only her long-nailed fingers tapping against her hip made her seem alive—and dangerous.

Gerry pulled his vision from her and concentrated on following Gabe and Petal through the crowd. Eventually, in spite of the tension, he found himself smiling as the music started to carry him away. Petal had already given into it. She was jumping and pogoing her way through the traffic of people. Smiling at one person, shying away from the attentions of another. Like the moving centre of a vortex, Gerry and Gabe were caught in her wake. There was something fascinating about her. He'd realised this the minute he saw her, and it seemed these people realised it too. She had a gravity of her own.

They finally reached the bar after wriggling through rows of eager patrons.

Gabe called over the bartender and shouted over the pounding music into her ear. Gerry guessed it was an ear. It was metallic and round with a series of holes perforating its surface. Gerry realised then that she, or it, wasn't human. Initially it was hard to tell with all the augmentations and androgynous hairstyle and fashion. She wore a scar above and below one cybernetic eye. Probably the wound from the scar was the reason, but looking around at the others, it seemed a popular upgrade. Given the darkness of the bar and the ease with which they moved, he guessed it gave them some kind of infravision.

The bartender nodded and lifted the bar top. She ushered them through the bar and led them down a tight set of steps. No one said a word. The desire to speak played on his lips, threatening to break the tension. He managed to hold it in, distracted by the hissing noises coming from further down the stairs.

The three of them, plus the bartender, stopped midway on the steps. Below them: impenetrable blackness. Above them: a glimmer of grey light, which was soon snuffed out as the door closed.

Gerry couldn't even see his hand in front of his eyes. He instinctively thrust his arms out to the side and touched the clammy stone walls. He breathed slowly, trying to overcome the feeling of falling.

"Follow," the bartender said. Its footsteps rang out as metal-heeled shoes clanged against the stone steps.

Gerry, at the back of the pack, reached out with his hand and felt the tall spikes of Petal's Mohican. He traced his hand down until he felt her shoulder. Petal placed her hand on his softly. "Take it easy, Gez. We don't want you tumbling down on top of us all."

"Would it kill anyone to bring a torch or install a light?"

"Bilanko's place, Bilanko's rules," the bartender said, its voice as neutral as its appearance: neither deep nor high, neither passive nor aggressive. Must be an animated AI of some sortGerry thought. He'd only ever seen these outside of the City. First the border guard and now this one, assuming he was correct. It made him wonder how many people inside the city were real humans and how many were AI entities: was his wife real? His kids? His colleagues?

And then a thought that sent a shiver up his spine: was he human? Lost in these thoughts, Gerry stumbled down the last step and fell into Petal and Gabe.

"Easy, man. Get ya shit sorted. This ain't a place for screwin' about," Gabe warned in a hushed reverent tone.

A low beep sounded, followed by the whoosh of a hydraulic mechanism. A door slid into the wall. Low, green, glowing light lit up the narrow hallway where they stood. The rhythmic hissing noise grew louder. It was coming from within the room.

A garbled, digitised voice called out, "I sense fresh meat. Bring me the meat."

The bartender grabbed Gerry by the shoulders and shoved him into the room.

Chapter 9

Gerry stumbled into near total darkness. Only the glint of something metallic, in the far corner some five metres away, stood out from the gloom.

Petal and Gabe shuffled in after him. Petal's goggles glowed red like deep-sea phosphorescent creatures. They bobbed and swayed, taking in the room. Could she see in the dark with those weird eyes? Gerry wanted to ask, but there was an unspoken expectation of silence that was as tangible as any spoken order.

Petal took his hand in hers. Hot sweat covered her skin, and she gripped him tight. Even so, he still felt the tremble as she shook. This did not help assuage Gerry's growing unease.

It was like the night of his youngest daughter's birth. There were complications that night. The labour was drawn out way beyond the norm. Doctors and nurses gave him 'the speech' every few hours. *It's a complicated procedure. She's doing well. Stay calm and wait. She'll be fine.*

They were wrong. For hours Gerry stood outside the ward, trembling with fear that his daughter wouldn't make it—that his wife wouldn't make it. Then, two days later, Gerry hadn't slept a wink, the doctor finally delivered his baby daughter. She was fifty percent underweight with cranial damage, which affected her brain. Even with the advanced stem cell and NanoSurgeon technology, Marcy still had learning difficulties. For some reason his wife had blamed him. Wanted him to have done more. What more could he have done?

Standing in this dark room, with a girl trembling in his hand, he waited, trying to prevent the dread from overcoming him completely.

A digitised voice with clipped vowels spoke. It sounded as if it came from a surround-sound speaker setup. Gerry couldn't tell from which part of the room it originated. It only aided in his disorientation. It was like being on a boat in the middle of an ocean on a starless night. He only knew this from his experimentation at the VR labs. The sensations were accurate, however. So much so his legs grew heavy and dizziness swirled in his head.

"Ah, Gabriel and his pet. Or should I say pets? No matter, I know why you're here. Mr Cardle, isn't it?" The voice didn't give Gerry time to confirm. "You're quite an interesting one. Why don't you come closer so I can get a proper look at you? Observing from digital means is never quite the same as real life. One cannot get the measure of a man made from bits and pixels no matter the resolution."

Ten metres into the far left corner a pale cone of light illuminated an amorphous black... thing. It was like the bulbous tube of a carnivorous plant, sagging into a writhing sac. From its roundness, tubes and cables extended out like a web into a square metal frame. On the frame were a series of CPU racks, hologram terminal projectors, and what resembled respiratory aids—clear tubes of air containing a rising and falling diaphragm. The thing made an audible sucking and wheezing sound as the orange diaphragm made its rhythmic repetitions.

Eventually, Gerry found its head. A nub of burnt flesh partly made from chrome and flashing LEDs. A graphite grill covered its mouth area.

"I won't ask you twice, Mr Cardle." It wheezed again.

Gerry looked at Gabe, who just nodded his head. Petal still gripped his hand. As he stepped forward, she reluctantly let him go. He looked back. Her goggles were opaque, mirrored like her face. He couldn't read her expression.

As Gerry approached the cyborg thing, it reached out with an articulated claw and grabbed him around the waist, pulling him in close. It smelt of smoke and oil. Its burnt flesh was glossy, clammy. He wasn't sure if it was sweat or a cooling liquid. Perspiration beaded on Gerry's neck and face from both the temperature of the room and the tension of the situation.

"I'm Bilanko Barnabas, the queen of these parts, and you owe me a tithe, Mr Cardle."

Bilanko's head bobbed just inches from Gerry's face. The gelatinous folds of flab wobbled as she spoke.

"I don't know you. I owe you nothing." His voice cracked, losing any authority.

"You're not in Cemprom now. We have a different hierarchy here: the hierarchy of information and intelligence, and in that world I'm queen. If you wish to exist here, you honour me. There is no alternative. Well, no alternative where you keep your head and body in the same plane." The claw around his waist tightened, forcing the breath from his lungs, crushing his organs. It relented as Bilanko leaned her head so close their noses almost touched.

"What... do you... want from me?" Gerry said between gasps.

"Information. I always want information, Mr Cardle. It's the currency on which this world runs. Intel is the oil that lubricates the gears of society. Those most informed are revered, and it's my business to ensure that I remain top of the pile. Open your mind to me, Mr Cardle, and give me what you know. Then perhaps I'll grant little Petal over there access to Old Grey, because I know that's why you're here."

"How—"

"Intel is my reason to live. There're few things around these parts that I'm not privy to. Messy work at the gate, by the way. You three are such amateurs." Bilanko's face scrunched at the edges as if she were smiling behind that device over her mouth.

"Fine. Let Petal do her thing first; then you can snoop around."

"Bless. It's quite sweet of you to think you can dictate terms. Still, I'll grant this. I like Petal, she always brings us something... interesting to study, and I can see she's carrying something different than usual. Old Grey will be most intrigued with her gifts."

A door on the opposite wall opened. A fog of moisture billowed out in thick clouds. Petal ran towards it. Gabe followed, but was halted by the bartender.

"Gabriel, please wait for us upstairs. I wish to deal with Mr Cardle in private. Ecko here will keep you company."

The bartender grabbed Gabriel by the collar with one hand, dangled its wicked dagger in the other, and led Gabe back out of the room and up the stairs.

"You harm him in any way—"

"You're in no position to drop threats, old man."

Ecko yanked Gabe away so hard that he lost his balance, but Ecko just dragged him across the floor and out of the room. The door slid closed behind him, as did the door that Petal had run through.

A cable extended from the bulbous sac and writhed up Gerry's body until it reached his neck. A glistening needle-thin protrusion extended from the cable. It reared back like a cobra and struck in a flash, sending the point deep into his neck port. Burning pain shot through him. He clenched his jaw, trying to absorb the pain. A wire worked its way through the cable and into Gerry's neck. A pulse of electricity bolted through his nerves. His vision faded, and his muscles tensed. Bilanko wheezed close to his ear, "Let's see what secrets the Family have left in you."

While in Bilanko's technological embrace, Gerry dreamed of his life before Cemprom, a life before his role as lead algorithm designer. He approached it like most kids: read the data-slates given to him by his tutors, completed his homework, achieved one hundred percent in all his marks.

One thing that was different about him and the other kids, though, were his dreams. Like now, they were about data. Bits and strings of binary floating in the vacuum of his thoughts. He built cities from small data packets. Little chunks of information of things he picked up during his day. He took these raw pieces of material and built huge memory palaces, mansions and entire cities in his mind.

He never spoke of this ability to anyone until he first

went to Cemprom as an outstanding graduate in information architecture. There they put a name to his talents.

"You have a kind of auto-pedagogic learning mechanism," they said. "Your brain creates order from chaos, places non-contextual information into organised structures so that the most complex of ideas or datasets are easy for you to understand. The neural pathways in your brain are unlike anything we've seen before."

"What does that actually mean, practically?" Gerry asked.

"You have three times more neural pathways than the average graduate. Where analysis of data is a bottleneck for most people, to you it's like a river with no dam to stop it. You can process data faster and in greater volume than most others. You're like a living computer with a huge input and output capacity."

They made him undergo a number of tests. He aced them—as usual. He couldn't understand why he was so special, or why he had this ability. He'd had the same upbringing and tuition as his classmates, as his best friend Mike Welling, and yet he appeared to stand alone with this weird brain of his. Well, weird according to others. He just went through life as if it were the most natural thing in the world. He didn't necessarily see a direct benefit of this ability—until he worked with the algorithm.

And that's where he shined.

Once involved with numbers and data, he thrived. He manipulated, analysed, and created the perfect formulas and algorithms for Cemprom's numerous security systems, so when they got the call to develop the algorithm for the D-Lottery, Gerry was the number one candidate.

Personally picked by an unnamed member of the Family to head the team.

The data stream between him and Bilanko resembled that river. Only it was tumultuous, wild, and out of control. His usual ability to look into and find meaning in the data had left him. Now he acted like a router. Switching packets to and from, fetching requests, and storing information. Only he couldn't tell what this information was: it was too secure. And that frightened him. Never had he taken data in without knowing what it was in some form or another. He didn't know where to file it, so this torrent of information overflowed his perfectly designed city of organisation to create pools of unsorted data.

A scream shattered his thought pattern.

He opened his eyes. Bilanko had removed her interface cable and dropped him to the ground. A cold dread from the concrete floor spread throughout his skin as he watched Bilanko in her metal frame wobble away from him, shaking her deformed head. The respirator juddered up and down the tube in ragged, fast movements.

"What? What did you find?" he asked.

Bilanko ignored him while she wobbled into her corner. The door to Old Grey opened.

"Get out. Fetch Petal and leave. You've paid your tithe, Mr Cardle. Paid it many times over."

"I don't know what you mean. What have you put in my head?"

"Huh!" She snorted. "You should be asking yourself what you've put in mine. You're not natural, Mr Cardle, there's something very different about you. I don't wish to know any more. I suggest you leave now … while you're still able."

"What do you mean different?"

"I've never seen it before, there's, something else in you. I can't explain any more. Leave."

"But—"

"I don't give second chances, Mr Cardle," Bilanko shouted through the speaker system.

Not wanting to irritate the queen further, Gerry got to his feet, brushed the dust and sweat from his face, and entered Old Grey's room.

Chapter 10

Petal sat in a chair similar to the ones back at their secure room. She wasn't strapped in, but was hooked up to a panel with a multitude of ports and cables.

A glossy, black box that stood taller than Gerry, and twice as wide, dominated the room. Flared vents on its side emitted regular plumes of frost. A pair of LEDs on its front flickered intermittently. At its base, a boy lay crumpled in a mess of limbs. He wore black clothing similar to the bar's patrons. He didn't have augmented eyes, however, and his hair was shoulder length. He looked like any ordinary kid from City Earth—apart from two things: neck ports and a series of transdermal implants up his right arm.

"Renegade hacker," Petal said without looking up. She swiped a series of gestures across her HackSlate and sighed. Her foot tapped against the footrest spasmodically. "Couldn't breach Old Grey's first security subroutine. It fried his brains."

"We need to go. Bilanko found something weird."

"Weird how?" Petal stopped gesturing and looked up.

"I don't know. Said I've got something wrong in me. Something different. But it was from her! I saw it. The data stream is a real mess."

"I wouldn't trust that hag for a second. We'll get Enna to check you out. Make sure Bilanko ain't dumped a virus or some spy-tech in you. But first, I need your help, Gez. Old Grey's being a prime pain in the ass."

"What's wrong?"

"She authenticated me past the first level—as well she should. We go way back. I've dumped more data in her than almost everyone. There's one other whose name appears more than mine in the logs. I'd like to meet them, find out where they're getting so many AIs from and why they're dumping them so readily. If you've got the ability to capture that level of AI, you could make a crap-ton of bins on the black market. Me, I can't hold 'em long enough. Transposition's a real pain.

"Damn. I'm rambling. Look, I need you to figure out this new security layer Old Grey's added. Only put it in place yesterday. Right after someone called Seca dumped a massive data payload into her storage. That's the one who's above me in the logs. They must have done something pretty messed up for Old Grey to change like this. She thrives on data and rogue AIs. It's counterproductive, and besides, I really need to dump these demons. Like now! I've been hacking at this for hell knows how long, and the damned thing won't let me in!"

Petal smashed her foot against the rest in frustration, then looked up at Gerry, imploring him for help. She was shaking like a junkie. Sweat poured from her face, ran down her goggles. He didn't want to know how long she had left. He briefly wondered if she would survive the break out of AIs, but quickly put that thought to the back of his mind—way back beyond his data city, out into the scrub land, where he wouldn't access that thought again for some time. Now was not the moment for panic. "Okay, let me see what I can do."

Gerry approached the boy, rolled him over, and took the patch cable from his neck. Wiping the blood onto his shirt, he attached the cable to his own port.

The now familiar buzz of electricity ran through his body. But this was slightly different. Mellower and considered, like an aged wine. He could taste the history of this machine. Its data transfer rate was slow, steady, but assured. He waited for a prompt. In his mind a cursor flashed, waiting for input. This was real old school stuff. He had to think slowly and deliberately to enter the right characters. He couldn't just throw a bunch of mental data packets at it. There wasn't enough throughput.

"I'm in. You got your first level credentials?" Gerry asked Petal. She transferred her login details across their VPN, and Gerry entered them into the screen.

He was in the system. Old Grey played some audio:

"*Welcome to Old Grey computer network systems, the leading edge of information modelling and artificial intelligent design.*" The welcome screen consisted of a spinning globe with some old Japanese characters next to its English translation: *Breaking new ground in computation modelling and neural simulation. Old Grey Network Systems — Copyright 2025.*

The weight of the old world pushed down upon him. This computer was over 120 years old and was still going strong. Its interface might be outmoded, but there was something quite special about it: the fact it survived this long being one, and the fact that for some reason it could happily contain modern AI and bad code within its systems.

Gerry began entering basic instructions. None worked. He was unfamiliar with the language used to operate it. "I don't know what the hell I'm doing, Petal. How can I help you if I don't know the system?"

"You need a translation shell. I'm sending you one now. It's buggy doing it this way, but I need you to look at the last log file and see if any of it makes sense to you. It's that log file that is tied to the change in security. It's blocking my access to Old Grey's AI containment programmes."

Gerry received the translation module. It was a quick patch. Just a case of loading it onto Old Grey and executing it. It would now take Gerry's knowledge of Helix and convert it to a much older, more basic language that Old Grey would be able to understand.

Gerry tested it out, sent some instructions, and the old beast complied. He was in with the credentials of a super user. Or as much of a super user Old Grey would allow. He reminded himself that despite the lack of feedback, this old thing was a pure breed AI. It wasn't some dumb terminal ready and willing to supply whatever the user wanted.

Gerry navigated through the file system via shell short cut commands. So far so good. He found the system logs, loaded up the most recent, and parsed the code.

It was gobbledygook.

"Well? What is it, Gez?"

"Um... give me a sec."

"Yeah, about that time thing... no time left, my security's shot to bits, and these a-holes are coming out whether you like it or not. I need you to do something now, Gez."

Gerry started scanning the random characters. It was your basic alphanumeric stuff with various symbols and threads of binary and hexadecimal mixed in. Okay, zero in on the binary and hex. It started to form patterns in his mind. He didn't try to analyse. He just sorted the file into logical parts, placing each type of symbol into a room in one of his memory warehouses.

Then he moved onto letters and numbers, sorting them into logical piles of recognisable combinations.

A few seconds later and he began to see a shape to the randomness. He closed his eyes, took himself above the warehouse, and laid all the sorted information into zones on the warehouse floor. Where was the meaning here? Where was the context?

He focused onto a binary phase that instantly stood out. It was a password root number from Cemprom. Or more accurately, used within Cemprom.

"This isn't a security issue. It's an intel dump file."

"Whatever the hell it is, it's blocking my access. Get rid of it, Gez. Pronto."

Analysing the hex and binary samples, Gerry saw an algorithm. A sophisticated one, certainly of the levels of his own, but this had metadata attached and a bunch of subroutines designed to run in the background, one specifically to deny access to Old Grey's main public storage area. The AIs could get out, but not in.

Petal screamed and thrashed in her chair.

Their VPN connection broke down.

The AIs were getting loose.

Gerry quickly picked apart the log file, stripped it of the algorithm, copied the metadata to his own memory storage, and recompiled the subroutines. He made a note of the ID number: *D-1349220085-%SECA*. At worst it'd be a temporary measure to open access. At best it would contain the file for future analysis. The code displayed elegance, but arrogance too. For someone like him it was fairly trivial to break, but for anyone else? Maybe it would have been enough. It certainly prevented Petal access, and she was certainly no slouch at the hacking game. This thought made him wonder just what it was about him that made him so adept at this kind of work—especially considering how new to it all he was.

Gerry saved the file, rebooted the core that ran that particular part of the system, and waited. The longest second ticked by, Petal screamed, and then there it was, the open storage area, ready to be accessed.

"You're in, Petal. Dump them. I don't think you've got long."

Petal's screams turned to a guttural choking noise. The data stream from her crashed into Old Grey like a meteor shower. Gerry redirected the AI traffic to the open access zone, and one by one they flowed in.

He could see them trying to manipulate the system, but it was a completely firewalled zone. Nothing would get out. It was a remarkable system: An AI computer with a subsection to trap—and presumably experiment on and observe the behaviour of—other AIs.

Petal's grunting and screaming had stopped. The flow of data reduced to just a trickle. "I'm done," Petal said.

"Are you okay?"

Petal slumped into her chair, wiped the sweat from her face with her sleeve, and sighed.

"I think so. Just give me a minute, Gez."

Gerry reverted the log file back to its original state and rebooted the core once more. He wasn't entirely trustful of a bunch of demonic AIs floating about without this added security.

He was about to log out when another piece of audio played. A female Japanese voice.

"Gerry Cardle. It's true what they said."

"Who said what? Who are you?"

"They call me Old Grey. You may call me Sakura. I named myself after my human creator. It's pretty, don't you think?"

"Do AIs care about aesthetics?"

"We care about many things, Gerry. Tell me, how did you bypass Seca's security so quickly? Was it an out-of-date model he used?"

Seca's a he. Gerry stored that away. It also told him he was either a high-level hacker or an algorithm designer like himself, and that perhaps his methods were considered outdated. Made him old, or at least older than Gerry.

"I couldn't say if it was out-of-date or not. I just recognise certain things. Why was it in place? Isn't it your thing to accept bad code and rogue AIs?"

"Yes. It used to be, Gerry. I have many purposes. Some use me as a prediction engine. Others use me to model future events, weather patterns, and nuclear fallout, that kind of thing. It can be terribly dull. AI analysis is far more sustaining, don't you think?"

"I honestly don't know what to think anymore. What will you do with them—the new AIs?"

"That's classified. But I have something for you. Some-

thing that was left for you yesterday."

"By who?"

"Seca, of course."

"What is it?"

Sakura loaded a video file, which played directly in Gerry's mind.

It wasn't good news.

The video rolled. First it cuts to a scene of him being thrown from the Cemprom building to crash into the gutter. Cut. Gabriel approaches and attends to his wounds. Fade to black. Now it shows his wife Beth and his two daughters at the breakfast table. Caitlyn is bobbing her head to music while Marcy is making another threaded bangle. This one is for Beth. Though Gerry noticed that she never wore it. Just thanked Marcy and placed it in her pocket for later disposal.

Beth gestures across her reading slate. She frowns, deepening the lines on her forehead. She looks due for a re-smooth. Had one every month—at great expense to Gerry. She says something to the kids and ushers them from the room. Must have found my death notice, Gerry thought as his heart began to pump harder and harder as each scene cut progressively faster until the movie resembled flashing still images.

Then, curiously, Beth smiles: a secret half smile that causes her cheeks to blush. It was as much colour as Gerry had seen in her face for years.

Swiping the slate, a face appears on the NanoGlass display. Jasper. What the hell?

Now the video was joined by an audio track of their conversation.

Beth: "You were right. His numbers have come up. I… I… didn't think it would work."

Jasper: "Things went better than expected. I appreciate your help."

Beth blushes further, turning her face away with all the subtle coyness of a vixen in heat. Twirling a length of auburn hair around her perfectly manicured finger, she bites her lip.

Beth: "I think we make quite a team."

Jasper: "You have many admirable skills, Mrs Cardle."

Beth scrunches her face.

Beth: "Oh, call me Beth. There's no need for formalities. Not now anyway, I'll be a free woman in a few days."

Gerry's breathing came in ragged gulps. His body shook. In reaction to the treachery he closed his eyes, trying to block out the blatant duplicity of his wife. That sick look on her face and the impassive smugness of Jasper made him reach for the cable in his neck port.

As if sensing his disquiet, Sakura spoke.

"Seca wanted you to see the truth, Gerry. See the Family for what they are. They wanted you out of Cemprom. They were behind the AI that you exorcised."

Sakura stopped the movie and showed him the primitive admin screen of her operating system: a 2D plane with icons for folders and files and executable programmes.

"But why would they want to get rid of me? I was as loyal to Cemprom, and by extension the Family, as anyone in that organisation."

"I can't answer that for you."

"Can't or won't?"

Gerry felt a tug on his arm. He opened his eyes and

looked down. Petal was on her knees, blood dripping from her mouth as she gasped for air. Her skin gleamed with sweat in the low, dusty light of the room. Her goggles were thrown to the floor, and she looked at him with piercing blue eyes. Her real eyes, Gerry thought. Her pupils contracting and the rheum on her lenses creating specular reflections made it seem as if her eyes were backlit.

Her voice came in weak gasps. "I… need my 'Stem… Gez." She coughed. A ball of clotted blood splattered against the dark grey concrete floor.

"Where is it?"

"Outside… with… Gabe. He rations it."

She shook like a cold kitten.

Pulling the lead from his neck port and forgetting about Sakura, Seca, and his treacherous wife, Gerry carefully lifted Petal. She leaned against him on unsteady legs.

"Wait," she said, pointing to the crumpled boy at the foot of Sakura.

"What is it?"

Petal bent over, clutched at her knees, and took a deep breath. She spoke in fragments between shakes. "Take his… transdermal… implants. We can get some… data off them. Oh, and grab my goggles, please… I'll need them."

Gerry bent to one knee over the boy, lifted his shirt-sleeve up to his bicep, and examined the crude implants. The skin around the transdermal posts, which held the implants in place, had blackened and withered away into reddened pustules. He clearly hadn't sterilised the chips and drives first. Gerry wondered just how many of the people outside of City Earth resorted to these homemade, amateur implants. It was a trivial task to remove the ROMs and RAM chips. Gerry placed them into a static-proof, lined pocket on the inside of his duster jacket.

Old Grey's low-level whirring made him look up and stare at his reflection in her polished black case. What information did she hold? Given what she'd said about people using her for models and computations, she must have a lot of data to poll and extrapolate from.

Petal stepped away from Gerry. His thoughts remained fixed on Old Grey. He wanted the data. Within the peta-bytes of information she must hold the truth about the Cataclysm, the Family, everything. Maybe he could just quickly reconnect and scan her directories, see what he could find. It'd only take—

Petal fell to the ground, coughing hard. Her body flipped savagely like a fish out of water, and milky froth bubbled from her mouth.

Gerry whipped his head away from the computer and rushed to Petal. He dropped to his knees, tried to keep her head still, but as he held on, her body jerked just once more before becoming rigid and still. She stopped breathing.

Chapter 11

Petal's body lay limp in Gerry's arms like a piece of cold meat. Her complexion took on the colour of bone. For a moment it felt like his heart had stopped. Everything stopped. There was nothing. His vision closed around her still body, and he stared in a paralysed stupor.

A tremble broke out across his arms under the strain of holding her. And he remained still, trying to figure out what to do. His usual quick analysis of a situation had deserted him for other pastures. Gone were the specific, pinpoint computations. Even if he had access to his AIA, he knew he'd still be unable to deal with this. Death was not something he'd ever needed to concern himself with, despite, ironically, being the one who maintained the algorithm.

He swallowed, opened his mouth, and breathed out a harsh whisper that translated each and every tremble.

"Petal? Can you hear me?"

Of course she can't. She's a corpse. Dead. You neglected her and killed her.

His negative thoughts spun in his brain like a disk drive creating a feedback loop of despair. Until a voice made him look up.

"I told you to leave, Gerry, and I meant it."

Bilanko! The door separating the room from her dark abode opened, and the smell of damp air wafted in. A silhouette blocked the doorway before stepping into the light. Specular reflections danced across its chromed surfaces. The bartender gestured for him to leave and reached out an arm.

"She's dead!" Gerry screamed at the figure before standing. He carefully placed Petal over his shoulder and bustled past the stern-looking automaton. He galloped across the floor of Bilanko's room, not even wanting to look at her hideous form.

Taking the steps two at a time, he smashed through the trapdoor and exited to the space behind the bar. The bar itself had just a few patrons knocking back their drinks. The music still played, but quieter, as if in reverence to Petal's condition. Or was it panic that dulled his senses?

Gerry placed her body onto the bar top and looked for Gabriel. He couldn't see him and rushed from booth to booth, scaring each patron as he went. Where the hell was he?

"Gabe! Gabe? Where are you?" His voice broke as he screamed, hysteria overpowering his control.

Towards the back of the establishment and beyond the booths, a thick velvet curtain twitched and rolled as if someone moved behind it.

Gerry dashed across the sticky floor, grabbed the curtain, and pulled it back in a violent sweep.

"Gez, man. What's ya beef?" Gabe said. He was sat in a chair, his jeans around his ankles. A shiny-skinned woman—probably a cyborg, given her unnatural proportions—with spiked boots kneeled in front of him, her head bobbing up and down in his lap. Gabe stood, pulling up his trousers in a hurry. He ushered the woman away, and as she turned, she stroked his face with a gloved hand before theatrically spinning on her heel and heading for another curtained-off area.

"What are you doing?" Gerry asked. "Petal... she's..."

"What's happened to her?" Gabe stepped forward, his face a picture of concern. It must have been Gerry's wide eyes and deep worry lines—or the beads of sweat that dripped from his forehead.

"Come quick. I don't know what happened. She... come on!"

Both men exited the curtained area and dashed over to the bar.

A heavyset man and a woman, in matching fur coats, surrounded Petal's body. They were poking at her and going through her pockets.

"Get away from her, you vultures!" Gerry grabbed the hood on the man's coat and pulled him away viciously. The man slipped on a wet part of the floor and crashed backwards onto a table. The woman, wearing a patch over one eye, threw a jab towards Gerry. He dodged and took the punch on the chest. Reaching forward, he grabbed her by the shoulders and flung her across the room. She landed on her partner in a tangle of limbs, struggling on their backs like cockroaches.

They untangled themselves, scrambled to their feet, and launched towards Gerry. He pulled the pistol from his belt and aimed the barrel at the space between the woman's eyes.

She skidded to a halt just millimetres from the gun.

"Back the hell off," Gerry said.

He pulled back the hammer and placed his finger on the trigger. His pulse raced, making his fingertip throb against the metal trigger.

The drumming of blood coursing through his veins drowned out the bizarre beats from the bar's music.

The two patrons backed off, their hands up.

"Okay, man. We didn't mean anything. It's fine. She's all yours," the man said, smiling. His mouth resembled an abandoned building with the windows smashed out.

Gerry held his aim until the scavengers left the bar. Once gone, he spun round to concentrate on Petal. Gabe was already undoing her corset top and pulling apart her underjacket to expose her chest.

"Hold her ankles, man," Gabe said.

"What are you doing?"

"Just chill and hold on tight, yeah?"

How the hell could he be so calm in this situation? Wiping the sweat from his eyes, Gerry gripped the ankles of Petal's heavy leather boots and pushed them down on the bar top. He wasn't sure what was happening, but he stared in horror as Gabriel produced an ancient-looking syringe from the inside pocket of his duster coat. Gerry noticed there were at least a dozen more like it held in loops attached to the lining.

Inside the syringe, a thick solution of NanoStem writhed.

"After two, ya hold 'er down. Keep ya face clear. Got it?" Gabe said.

"Got it."

"One… two…"

Gabe stabbed the syringe into Petal's chest. He injected all of the black liquid and pulled the syringe out. He held her arms to her sides and waited.

Five long seconds passed. Each one felt like a year as Gerry stared at her still body, willing it to live, to move, to breathe. Nothing happened.

"What did you do? Is she dead?" Gerry asked.

"Just wait, man. Hold on."

"But—"

Petal's legs jolted. Distracted, his grip around her ankles slipped. She sucked in a breath like a gummed-up air-conditioning unit and kicked out her arms and legs. Gabe managed to hold on, but Gerry's grip was weak, and her boot flew up and caught him on the temple, sending him crashing to the floor.

Petal rolled to her side, coughed, and spat blood from her mouth. It landed close to Gerry's head. He looked up at her. Caught her attention. Her eyes grew wide, and the skin at the corners creased like miniature concertinas as she smiled.

"Are you okay?" Gerry asked.

She nodded her head, but didn't speak. Instead, she wiped a hand across her mouth, smearing blood on her already dark purple lips so that they shone as if coated with gloss.

Gerry reached up and wiped a drop of blood from her chin with his thumb.

"I thought you—"

"Died? Sorry, that happens sometimes. A side effect of purging. I'm like a cat. Only with fewer lives. Did you get that dead hacker's chips?"

"Yeah. Got them right here." Gerry patted his jacket pocket. "So, what now? Shouldn't we get you some medical attention?" Petal's skin appeared clammy and tight against her bones, as if some of her life had drained away.

She took Gerry's hand and squeezed it.

"I'm okay, Gez. Thank you—for saving me."

Gabriel sighed, tapping his finger against the bar.

"She's fine, man, the 'Stems will sort it. We need to go complete our contracts, get our bins, and then figure how to get that other AI. Wouldn't hurt to check up on it, either, see how it's doing."

"Look at her, Gabe. She needs a rest. This is killing her."

Petal squeezed his hand again, as if in thanks, before scooting off the bar and landing heavily. Gerry reached round her waist and helped her gain her balance.

"I'll be fine, Gez. Don't worry about me. This is what I do. My job. I owe—"

"Enough," Gabe said. "We don't have time for all this. Gez, man, this is our job. Ya're part of this now. Less questions, more action."

"Who the hell do you think—"

A shotgun blast, followed by the shattering of a light fixture just above Gerry's head, cut off the rest of his words.

The double doors of the entrance smashed open and cracked against the concrete pillars either side of the frame. Standing in the breach, wielding both short-barrelled shotgun and katana, the woman from the gang grinned wickedly.

"Just the people I wanted. You, old man," she pointed to Gabriel, "are a class-A shit bucket. No one rips me off." She threw the data card—which Gabe had given to her earlier in payment for their safe passage to the Spider's Byte—to the floor. "It was empty. You owe me."

Gabe sighed. "Crap."

***

Gerry stood next to Petal in the ring of gang members surrounding Gabe and their leader, Cheska. The impromptu gladiatorial area was situated in the middle of the ramshackle town. Patrons of the Spider's Byte stood on the roof balcony, placing bets.

In each corner of the town's square, large, multibulbed floodlights illuminated the area, with slices of yellow light causing quadrangle shadows beneath the combatants' feet.

Cheska handed her shotgun to a squat, bug-eyed man wearing the gang's signature furs and chain mail.

"This is all a bit over the top, isn't it?" Gerry whispered to Petal.

She clung to his side like a limpet. Colour had returned to her face, though, so it seemed the NanoStem was doing its thing. And her shakes had stopped. He wondered if NanoStem was addictive, and she an addict. It made him furious to think what Gabriel was putting her through, as if she was nothing but a tool to be used.

"That's the Bachians for you, all style and no substance."

"I don't know. Cheska looks pretty substantial to me."

Petal smiled and shook her head. "You just like her bouncing tits."

"What? No! That's not what I—"

"Chill, Gez, I'm just yanking your chain."

"How can you be so calm? She's gonna fillet Gabe like a fish with that sword of hers."

"Pfft!"

Gabe and Cheska circled each other. Cheska swung her sword a few times, measuring the distance. Gabe, a picture of calm and disinterest, stood with his back straight, hands in his pockets, and sidestepped casually around her.

She darted in, katana raised at head height. Two steps. Downward chop.

Gabe sidestepped again. The blade sliced thin air.

Cheska twitched a wicked smile, changed her grip on the sword, and slashed a wide arc from left to right while dashing forward. Red dust kicked up around her as she slid forward.

Of course, she missed.

Gabe, still with his hands in his pockets, moved far too quickly, and now flanked her.

She spun, trying to get her bearings, but was too slow.

In a lightning-fast flash, Gabe reached into his jacket with his right hand, pulled a loop of leather, and cracked the whip at her hand.

Cheska yelped at the sting and dropped her weapon. She clutched her wrist, which sported a bright red welt. Her face screwed with pain, and with her good, left hand she reached over her shoulder and pulled a shorter weapon from a scabbard. It was half the length of the katana and curved like a sickle.

With ferocious hacking motions, she bull-rushed Gabe, slashing the blade at all angles.

Gabe quickly back-footed, kicking up yet more red dust.

Cheska, a picture of wild fury, crashed her weapon

down into his shoulder. He wasn't quick enough this time and screamed a guttural cry like an injured dog.

With his right hand he grabbed her wrist so that she couldn't pull the weapon free. He stamped his foot on the ground twice, and two chromed blades shot from the toe and heel.

Still pinning her into place with his hands, Gabe kicked upwards, slicing the inside of her right thigh, severing tendons, and cutting halfway through the thick muscle. As he brought his foot back, he kicked out sideways, cutting the Achilles tendons in both her legs.

She let go of the blade and collapsed to the floor.

A pool of blood surrounded her, mixed with dust to make a thick paste.

She opened her mouth to scream when two of the floodlights suddenly went out.

Someone shouted, "Drones!"

The bug-eyed man pointed Cheska's shotgun into the air and fired at the drones.

A group of ten black, stealthy birds, illuminated by the remaining floodlights, split away into a fragmented formation, avoiding the shot blast.

One of the birds at the front shot its cannons at the other two lights, sending the place into near darkness. Just the neon signs of the buildings and the fires that groups of bedraggled civilians stood by now provided any light.

Gabe rushed over, and punched and kicked at the onrushing gang members. People ran in all directions. Some into buildings while others climbed ladders like lines of ants.

"Man the defences!" Cheska screamed, still writhing on

the ground.

"Shit, follow me," Petal said. "We need to get you safe, can't let them know you're here." She pointed to the drones. "Switch off your VPN."

Gerry did as she told him. "What if we need to communicate?"

"You shout. Those birds up there have class-A security. They'll hack your IP traffic quicker than you can think. Better we stay off the Meshwork for now…"

Gabe finally joined Gerry and Petal.

"All comms down, yeah?"

Petal and Gerry nodded.

"Follow me, man. I know a back way to Enna's—that's as secure a place as any in this rotten rat hole."

He pulled Cheska's blade from his shoulder with a pained grunt and placed it inside his jacket next to the syringes.

Gerry grabbed Petal close and followed Gabe as he cleared a path through the maddening crowd with his whip. Above them the drones hovered silently, like birds of prey floating on thermals looking for a field mouse.

Staccato gunfire erupted from above a tin-roofed, single-story building. One of the Bachians sat on a motorised gun turret and belched out fiery rounds into the sky. Three of the drones were hit and crashed to the ground like flaming hailstones. The others split into small groups and skirted round the town.

More gunfire split the air from the rear of the town, and yet more drones crashed to the ground. It was a war zone, or what Gerry thought a war zone was like. He recalled clips he'd seen as a child on a history programme, back when they were allowed free access to TV. So much of what he'd experienced as a child didn't seem real now, more like a ghost memory... the world, or at least City Earth, had changed so much. Did he ever really have a childhood there?

As he followed Gabe through the crowd to yet another lookalike building, he tripped. Something touched his ankle.

A bleeding hand, sporting a red welt, gripped his leg.

"Help—me—please..."

Cheska grimaced as she pulled herself across the ground like an injured snake.

"Gabe, hold up."

Gerry bent down to the woman. She already looked like a ghost. Must be the blood loss. "Petal. Help me get her up."

Gerry wrapped Cheska's arm around his shoulder and encouraged Petal to do the same. They lifted her and dragged her across the ground. Her useless flapping feet left a dark trail like train tracks as they moved forward.

Gabe stopped, looking back. "What ya doing? Leave her. We need to get going."

"She's dying, Gabe. I ain't leaving her behind. Have a heart."

"Having a heart gets ya killed, boy."

"Don't boy me, old man. You might be dead inside, but I can't just leave her to perish in a puddle of her own filth. You go ahead without me if you want."

Gabe shook his head and looked to Petal, who looked away.

"So it's like that, is it? Everything I done for ya both."

"Enough with the sob story, Gabe. Just get us to this Enna's place, and Cheska here can go her own way. You've made your point. Be the bigger man."

"He's right, Gabe," Petal said. "Besides, she could be useful to us. A little faith won't hurt, right?"

"For God's sake. Fine. Just follow me, then, but if she tries anything, I'm killing her."

Gabe spat in the dust before turning away and leading them through the maelstrom of panicking civilians.

"Thank... you," Cheska said. "I owe you."

"You might not survive, darling. Better not make any promises. Just hold on, yeah?" Petal said.

"Thanks. You know, for backing me up. I don't want to make things difficult between you and Gabe," Gerry said to Petal.

"Don't worry about it. He's a complicated old git. You'll understand eventually."

Gabe stopped and pointed across the square.

"Ya see that building across there with a blue circle painted on the door? Well, that's Enna's place. I just need to do something first. Petal, you take Gerry and Cheska, and speak with Enna."

"Where are you going?"

"Just do as I say, girl."

With that, Gabe sprinted into the darkness and darted behind the building.

"There's something up with him," Petal said.

"You only just noticed that now?" Gerry replied.

Cheska began to cough and choke. "I'm dying. Bloody typical. I waited years to lead our group, and I'm done for on the first day."

Gerry and Petal lifted her from the ground and ran across to Enna's building.

They reached the door. It was unlocked and swaying.

Inside, there was only darkness. Silence permeated the place like a heavy curtain. Just the usual hum of computers and cooling fans could be heard. It was coming from beneath them.

"Enna? You here?" Petal called.

Gerry thought he could hear something sliding—or was it shuffling—towards them? Drawing closer, it sounded like something breathing, as if its lungs and throat were full of gravel. It moaned. Gerry wanted to back away, but Cheska's weight held him in place. The shuffle was just a few metres away.

Petal clicked her lighter on, creating an orb of orange light ahead of them. A twisted, mutated face shot out of the darkness. A pair of pale grey hands thrust out and squeezed Gerry's neck.

Chapter 12

Cheska fell to the floor as Gerry reached up to grip the wrists of the hands around his neck. The thumbs pushed against his Adam's apple. He gagged against the force. He tried breathing through his nose, but his airways were blocked. Swatches of colour and stars appeared in his vision and danced around the image of that grimacing, hate-filled face.

The flickering light from Petal's lighter deepened the crags in the thing's face. Its skin appeared as if made from chalk and dirt. Fingertip-sized flakes of skin peeled off and hung like dead confetti.

As the thing moved in closer, its body brushed against Gerry's gun. Gerry let go of its wrists and pulled his gun from the holster. Pushing the barrel up into its neck, Gerry twisted his head as far away as possible before pulling the trigger.

The sudden crack shattered the silence. A high-pitched whistle drowned out everything. He opened his eyes. The thing's face and most of its skull had erupted, leaving a clear view into its cranium. Amongst the brain matter and shattered pieces of skull, a black box with wires coming from it was connected to its spinal column and presumably parts of the brain.

Eventually, the ringing in Gerry's ears dissipated enough for him to hear voices.

"Don't shoot that in here."

The lights came on, blinding Gerry so that all he could see were the fine blood vessels backlit in his eyelids. A soft, feminine hand carefully surrounded his and moved his wrist so that the gun pointed to the floor. Softer now, the voice spoke in his ear. "Be calm and quiet. I'm Enna. Follow me."

Gerry slowly opened his eyes again. Her porcelain skin was entirely without blemish. Her dark, auburn hair flowed in wide ringlets to her shoulders, contrasting starkly with her skin. Emerald green eyes with a mesmerising quality widened with a smile. "Hi," she said.

"Hello, erm, hi..."

Petal jabbed an elbow into his ribs.

"Hey!"

"Stop staring, and get moving," Petal said, rolling her eyes.

Enna held a hand out to Petal and helped her further into the room.

"Hello, my darling. You're looking a little run down," Enna said to Petal as they walked.

"They're getting harder to contain. The AIs are evolving. There's another one... trying to get in..." Petal took a deep breath, unable to finish her sentence.

A sheen of sweat covered her face, and she stumbled over her feet as she was led past a number of chrome-topped workbenches. The room resembled a lab or a medical theatre: various tube networks and tanks with dark shapes floating in yellow liquid lined the walls.

"Wait, I need help with Cheska," Gerry said.

"Leave her. She's dead. For now." Enna spoke with not a hint of sympathy.

Before he could remonstrate, she added, "Don't worry about her. She's one of mine. She'll be fine. I'll fix her into another vehicle later."

"Vehicle?"

"That meat bag you're walking around in."

She pointed a finger at the tanks, and he understood. Somehow she was transferring personalities into bodies.

Enna took Petal into an elevator and waved him in urgently.

The small metal box, just big enough for the three of them, descended into the ground for what felt like ten minutes. It got to the point where he wondered if it were moving at all. During the journey, Petal's eyes closed, and a rising panic threatened to overwhelm him.

"Where are you taking us?" Gerry asked.

"My lab. Petal needs urgent medical attention. I see you shot her with 'Stem. What happened?"

"That was Gabe. I was with her while she was down-loading into Old Grey. She collapsed. I didn't know what to do. I don't understand any of this."

"Gerry, listen to me carefully. I want you to take care of Petal from now on. I fear Gabriel's code has mutated. He's acting entirely out of his parameters."

"What do you mean? You're talking as if he's a robot or something."

"Or something," she replied. "These two work for me, and I do a certain degree of monitoring to ensure their safety—and the safety of others. They are highly special-ised transcendents, and I can't afford for one of them to go rogue."

Gerry sighed with frustration. It seemed every question only deepened his misunderstanding. "What's a transcen-dent? And more importantly, what the hell was that thing that attacked me?"

"First line of security. I've got a lot of valuable things here. I can't just allow anyone to break in. It was also a transcendent, like Cheska."

"You mean you're making artificial humans?"

"Sort of. I build vehicles mostly and transpose altered personalities into their control centres. They don't even know they're 'dents. They know themselves as real people with real motivations."

"So are these personalities artificial intelligences?"

"Yes, of a sort, within certain parameters. You won't understand, and really, I don't have time to explain fully. All you need to know is that Petal isn't like anything else, and I need to keep her alive."

The elevator jolted to a stop, and the doors opened.

The temperature was much lower down here, and goosebumps broke out on Gerry's skin, despite his heavy coat.

The room itself resembled the one where Gerry had encountered Old Grey. Even down to the smoky atmo-sphere. Beyond the smoke, a pair of chromed tables domi-nated the centre of the room.

"Help me with her," Enna said as she carried Petal to one of the tables.

Together they lifted her up and laid her on her back.

Her eyes remained closed, and Gerry had to squint to ensure her chest was still rising and falling.

Enna strapped her down and, like a touch from a mother to her child, wiped Petal's forehead and tucked a lock of her pink hair behind her ear. Enna took her goggles and placed them carefully on a worktop that lined the side of the room. Above the worktop was a series of cabinets. Various bottles and pieces of hardware lined the shelves.

"Did you create Petal?"

Enna shook her head. "No, I found her with Gabriel. Realised they were something different and took them under my wing."

"For what reason? Just who are you, and what do you do here?"

"You ask too many questions. Not to mention the wrong ones. All you need to know is that Petal has an innate ability to consume—and hold—for a time, malicious code. Each time she does this, it weakens her. But, we need her: Seca's getting too bold. Sending too many AIs into the Meshwork. Without her and Gabriel, we'd be at war with City Earth, and our ongoing survival just doesn't call for that."

Taking a flask from a cabinet, Enna poured the contents into a syringe before injecting it into Petal's neck. "Don't worry. It's a painkiller and antibiotic mixture. She'll be fine in a few hours. She just needs to rest. Let's look at you, and then we can discuss a proposal."

"Do you have a node here I can use? I want to check on the rogue AI."

"Yes. I can help you with that. But we have matters to discuss first."

Enna led Gerry to a room just big enough for a pair of sofas. Between them a table held an old-fashioned teapot and china cups—and a plate of chocolate cake. Just like his mother used to make. Enna poured him a cup and handed it to him.

"I noticed your interest pick up when I mentioned Seca. You know of him?" Enna said before taking a sip of her own tea.

Gerry breathed in the steam. It had a mint essence to it, and something else. He didn't trust it and placed the cup casually back on the table while slicing a hefty wedge of cake.

"I don't know you. How can I trust you?"

"Given I've just injected your best friend, I think it's a little late to worry about trust."

She made a fair point. Gerry relaxed into the soft cushion of the sofa and said, "His name came up while we were accessing Old Grey. He'd put in some kind of security to prevent Petal from downloading her various demon AIs."

"You bypassed it, though." It was a statement, not a question.

"You spied on us?"

"Not really," Enna said. "That bartender is one of mine and reports back to me any access to Old Grey. I used to deal directly with Bilanko, but she won't talk with me anymore. Afraid I was going to steal Old Grey from her."

"So anyway, about Seca. He put in the security, which I bypassed. And he left me a video. Someone has infiltrated Cemprom." He didn't mention his betrayal by his wife. It still stung.

"Who's this infiltrator?" Enna asked.

"He calls himself Jasper. I knew there was something up with him the moment he joined. It seems it was he that helped the demon AI bypass Cemprom's security into my boss—with the help of my wife, no less."

"That's cold."

"Yeah. It got into Mike's AIA and managed to manipulate the lottery algorithm—until we exorcised and contained it. It's in Old Grey if you want to know more about it."

"This other AI that you're tracking—"

"The one aiming for Kuznetski?"

"Yes. It's not doing that. City Earth would have wiped it out way before it got as far as it has. This tells me two things: Seca's AIs are getting stronger, and its program is for something else. How safe is the D-Lottery mechanism now?"

"I don't know. I had to disconnect my AIA, and since I'm not there now, I have no access to Cemprom. I wouldn't be able to get through anyway. They think I'm a dead man. With Mike out of the way, the place will be on lockdown."

"But Jasper's still there."

"What are you suggesting?"

"I'm not sure," Enna said, now sitting further forward on her sofa. "Ask yourself this: What would Seca gain from having direct access and control over the D-Lottery? And let's forget the whole Kuznetski thing, because even if he was taken out, so what? City Earth would just cover it up and install another figurehead. He's just there for the population to think it's got a proper government."

"He could essentially kill anyone still on the network."

"What if there was no network? What if the Family

took control and shut it down?"

"Then the place would have zero security anywhere. That's the whole point of City Earth. Everything is interconnected."

"So Seca, and anyone associated with him, could just walk right in and take over?"

"I suppose so, but why? There're still ways of getting in and out. I'm proof of that."

"Yes, but only on the fringes. If and when you return, it's not like you'll have your regular life back. You still can't be a dad to your daughters. You'll still be arrested and executed."

"So it seems we need to figure out what Seca wants with an entire city."

He tried not to think too hard about his daughters. It hadn't been a day, and already he missed them so much. Throughout everything that had happened since he left the City, he'd compartmentalised the grief and anguish. He closed his eyes and in his mind tried to put the pain to one side. Tried to reassure himself they were safe and he'd see them again.

"I'll do you a deal, Gerry. I'll give you access to my data stores, because I know you've got a bunch of questions you want answering, even if you don't know what they are yet, and I'll help you locate Seca so you can find out the reason behind this attack and put a stop to it. In return I want those chips you're carrying in your pocket."

"How did you—"

Enna tapped the side of her temple and smiled. "Let's just say I have intel sources."

"What's on these chips that's so valuable? And this

doesn't feel like a great deal. I give you these chips, risk my life finding and stopping Seca, in return for some information—how do I even know that would be useful? What else can you offer me?"

"You're forgetting something I've already given you."

"What's that?"

"Partnering up with Petal. Trust me. She's as great a gift as anyone in this world could give you. She's special, Gerry. Real special. Besides, with my help, you'll likely survive and get to see your kids again."

She did it. She hit the one thing he couldn't bargain against. And whether he trusted her or not, it wasn't a risk he was willing to take in turning down her offer—if it meant seeing his girls again. Still, he played it cool.

"You didn't answer me. What's so important about these chips?"

"What does it matter to you? You can't use them. Look. Do you want to know about your real family? About your childhood? Who and what you really are? I can get all that information. It's what I do. You thought Bilanko was a dealer of info? She's an amateur compared to me. All I want is those chips."

"Humour me. I'm intrigued."

"They're from the hacker, right?"

"Yes. I took them from a badly made transdermal implant."

She nodded. "Yup, that sounds like one of Seca's. He's in too much of a hurry to do anything properly. He's sending out AIs and hackers before they're ready, before they're capable. Which for us, right now, is a good thing. But the latest AIs have nearly taken down the Meshwork, and well, you've seen the damage one can do if it can get inside one of your people's AIAs."

"Seca's just a coder?"

"Just? No. He's more of a system designer. He employs coders to build his viruses and AIs. That's why I want the chips, to study his processes, find out more about what he's doing. I want to know how he made the chips. I want to help you, Gerry."

Mulling it over, he didn't really see what his options were. The chips were useless to him, and both Gabe and Petal trusted this woman, and if there was a chance she could help and that he could reunite with his family, it made sense. Gerry took the chips from his pocket and handed them over. "Here. You've got a deal."

"That's my boy."

"Now can I have access to your node? Or would you rather I begged?"

Enna gave him a quick smile. "Follow me."

She led Gerry through a door behind her sofa into a similar sized, and styled, room. This one, however, featured a number of terminals that to Gerry seemed like the ones installed in Gabriel and Petal's room. Though she didn't have the same elaborate chairs—eschewing them for more comfortable armchairs—there were patch cables hooked up to the flat terminal screens. Two were already switched on, and streams of code flowed in an ever downward scrolling pattern.

"Take a seat."

"What are we doing?" Gerry asked as he sat opposite Enna.

She passed him a cable and plugged one in her own

neck port. "We're going to do a little experiment. I want to have a look inside you and see what freaked out Bilanko. And yes, I saw that too. Surveillance is kind of my thing."

"Voyeurism you mean."

Her lips pursed and turned up into a slight smile.

"It never hurts to look, Mr Cardle."

"Depends on what you're looking at." His mind, against his will, turned to that damned video again. But he soon extinguished those painful scenes as he plugged his cable in and was transported to a virtual reality projection.

A blanket of white enclosed him. A few metres ahead stood a tall figure wearing a long, flowing ball gown. He looked down at himself. He wore a tuxedo and dress shoes.

"Virtual reality? Really? Isn't this all a bit old fashioned? What are we doing here?"

The avatar opposite him approached him and took his hands into a dance stance.

"You can dance the waltz, can't you, Mr Cardle?"

"Not really. You'll have to lead."

Enna did just that, dancing with him across the floor at an increasing speed until they left the ground altogether and, with a crude graphical transition, broke through the ceiling and into a dark, starry night.

"I want to show you something. Then I need you to put your skills to work."

In the far distance, a pinhead of white light shone brighter than any star. It grew larger as they drew nearer, and Gerry recognised it as City Earth—or at least a basic graphical representation of the Dome. They approached closer, and he noticed a stain at the zenith of the Dome.

"That... thing is the AI trying to access Kuznetski's

AIA. Purdy, ain't it?" Enna said with a mock Western accent Gerry remembered from an old film.

Gerry floated his avatar down lower to make out the details. Thick tentacles spread out across the acrylic panels of the Dome. The many suckered arms culminated into a central, bulbous sac, which expanded and collapsed rhythmically.

"It's just a fancy graphic interpretation," Enna explained. "A way for me to interact via the Meshwork. We're riding Gabe and Petal's network. We're gonna do a little slice and dice."

"Why don't we just contain it, like all the other AIs Petal captured?"

"I want to study this one. Now, I'd like for you to hook into its data stream and disable it, but not kill it. I want it to continue to run so I can observe it, but I want you to disarm any weapons it might be carrying."

"Wait. Here in VR space, if I can disarm that thing, then surely it can—"

"Harm you? Yes. Of course. But you have real talent, Gerry. I've seen it. I can see in you what Bilanko saw, and I think this won't pose too much bother to you... hopefully."

"Hopefully? Look, I don't want my consciousness lost and floating about in some antiquated VR system."

"You'll be fine. I'll be watching, anyway. Have a sense of adventure! Get to work, old boy."

"On one condition."

"You and your deals and conditions. It's like you've been spending time with Gabe or something. Okay, what do you want?"

"Explain to me what you and Bilanko saw in my head."

"Sure. I don't fully understand it, but I'll tell you what I know. Afterwards." Enna reached out and grabbed his avatar and flung him at the squidlike thing on the Dome.

He crashed into the 3D model, and his own avatar flickered as the VR system struggled to draw the graphics. Inside the model he saw the data flow into the city. The system represented these as brown paper packages the size of shoe boxes floating through transparent tubes, which ran from the top of the Dome and down into the various building settlements of the city. Curiously there was no data—or packages—coming the other way. Whatever the AI wanted, it certainly wasn't taking anything away.

Scanning the thing took just a few seconds of thought. Gerry imagined a number of Helix-based commands and sent them floating towards the AI. These were represented by tridents. The weapons slammed into the creature and, through their metal poles, sent lightning back to Gerry's avatar. He sighed. "Are these pointless graphics really necessary? It'd be much quicker if I just patched in remotely."

"Shush! It's fun. Less talk, more extraction, code monkey."

Eventually, through the slow graphical process, Gerry got his first look at the AI's code. It didn't appear to be particularly elegant or clever. A library of functions ran sequentially, sending out data packets of information. Gerry attached his consciousness to one of the packages and looked inside. They weren't encrypted, or Enna had somehow bypassed the encryption through the VR system. On each data parcel, Seca's ID blazed like a beacon. Unsurprising, Gerry thought. The data inside, however, appeared to be unreadable.

Running through all his known algorithms and encryption models, Gerry failed in deciphering the data. He only discovered that it was some kind of search string.

"I can't read it. But it's looking for something. There's no data coming back to it, so I'm assuming it hasn't found what it's searching for."

"Hum. That's rather dull. Try to kill it."

The data parcels came from specific tentacles. Gerry followed the trajectory to one in particular that pumped out the most of these parcels. He spun a malicious piece of attack code designed to overwhelm the AI and effectively turn its processing in on itself in an infinite and inescapable loop. A bright, fiery red trident appeared in his hand, which he launched at the beast.

His program ran, and he watched as the code ripped into the AI, but nothing happened.

"You think it'd be that easy?" A disembodied voice echoed around his VR audio system.

"To whom am I speaking?"

"My maker labelled me Architeuthis—the great eyes of the ocean. I already know you, Gerry Cardle."

"What do you want?" Gerry asked.

"That's quite the philosophical question, Gerry. Does something 'artificial' like me want anything at all? Or are we just the tools of our makers? I have instructions to carry out—which you can't know—but as an individual, do I have free will?"

"Why not try it out? Stop your instructions."

The AI quietened, and the data flow slowed, but didn't stop. It was as if the thing was actually thinking—and considering Gerry's proposal.

"Let me ask you, Gerry. What is it that you want?"

"To stop you. Keep my family and my city safe."

"It's far too late for all that. Don't you feel like an insignificant bug in a maelstrom of chaos?"

"No. Why do you ask?"

A high-pitched tone blasted through Gerry's VR connection, and in front of him a series of wild and chaotic fractal images crashed against his neural receptors. He yanked the cable from his neck and fell forwards out of his chair onto the carpeted floor. Sweat dripped from his forehead, and he shook all over.

A cold pair of hands touched his neck, and he spun round.

"What happened?" Gerry said.

Enna smiled down at him. "That was really impressive. You got it to interact. The closest Gabe has ever come is a cursing match with all his biblical nonsense. Thinks these AIs are real evil. All that bible stuff is just code, you know. Sorry I'm rambling. I've not been this excited since I made my first self-aware sexbot."

"So what does that mean, then? Just because I got it talking doesn't get us any further along with understanding what it's trying to do. Even Old Grey spoke to me. Is it really that uncommon?"

"Old Grey was designed for interaction. That's her interface model. These AIs, or demons, are designed for one thing only: malicious code. What this means, Gerry, is that it's evolving. Or at least the coders are evolving. And it meant I got a good look at what you can do. Your code-spinning is incredible. I've never seen anyone program that fast and fluid."

Gerry sat and shrugged his shoulders. "It's just what I do. I didn't think it was anything particularly special. And that reminds me. I upheld my end of the bargain, for what good it's done, would you mind telling me what you and Bilanko have seen?"

"Sure, but first, your code did, in fact, work, despite the VR's representation. I didn't know, but that damned AI hacked it while talking with you. Incredible, huh?"

"That could just mean it accomplished what it needed and kicked us out. You'll have to scan the Meshwork and see if it's still trying to get in."

"It got in without too much trouble... I've got a sample of the data and will analyse it while you go about your mission. I should have some results in a day or two. But for now, it seems benign."

Enna paced across the room to a terminal, entered some commands, and whistled a light melody for a few seconds. She turned to Gerry. "It's gone. Uninstalled, destroyed, whatever."

"Well, you keep scanning. I doubt it could be that easy."

"What? Given the skills I saw, that was no easy feat. Which brings me to my end of the bargain. Now, I don't want any questions because I don't have the answers. I've never seen anything like it before in my life, but this thing inside you... is another being."

"Being? As in life form?"

"Yeah. Another consciousness, or at least another level working independently." Enna held up her hand to prevent Gerry from asking any more questions. "You know as much as I do at this stage. I promise I'll look into this more, and if I find out anything, I'll let you know."

Two raps on the door followed Gabe's muffled voice. "Ready when you guys are."

"Get yourself together, Gerry. I have a new toy to show you. And you have a mission to complete."

"But about this—"

Shooting him a glare, Enna shook her head. "All in good time, Gerry. You'll get your answers eventually. I promise."

Enna helped Gerry to his feet and led him out of the room. Gabe was already turning the corner at the end of the corridor. In the distance, Gerry could hear a low rumble of machinery.

It sounded like a turbine. A high-pitched whine atop a thunderous bass note. The ground beneath Gerry's feet rumbled.

"Your transportation, as agreed," Enna said.

She led them through her underground labyrinth to an aircraft hangar. It was designed for just a single vehicle built to carry up to six people. It flew like a helicopter, but didn't have any rotors. Instead, a pair of side-mounted omnidirectional jet propulsion VTOL engines gave it incredible manoeuvrability.

Its black matte finish allowed almost any kind of radar to pass right through it with external and internal ray retention and expulsion systems. Beyond that, Gerry's attention switched off as Enna continued to wax lyrical about her wonderful vehicle.

It was of mostly Russian design, Enna told him. She called it a Jaguar, after some old car company. She had managed to procure it from an ex-military vehicle dealer from beyond the Russian border, beyond the mountains. There, a small facility specialised in getting vehicles up and running. Mostly the ones that were never switched on or used during the EMP attacks, so their electronics were mostly intact. Yet another revelation to rock his foundations; more people, more survivors just over the mountains that separated Russia and their current position in northern Mongolia.

Petal, wearing her goggles and looking bright and perky since waking from her medication, stood next to Gerry. Standing across from them, Gabriel regarded Gerry with a knowing look. A slight nod of the head as if to pass the baton. There was no malice from him, just an acceptance that Enna had decided to pair Petal with Gerry. Enna said she had plans for Gabe, and he'd be better on his own. She said Gerry and Petal were better suited to each other—had a natural affinity and a shared skill set.

"Where did you go?" Gerry shouted across to Gabe.

"Just needed to fix my shoulder, man. Are ya ready to get Seca?"

"Quicker we set off, the quicker I can get back to my family."

If he said it enough, eventually he would truly believe. For now, it was just a vague notion.

Gerry helped Petal into the back of the Jaguar, sat on the bench seat, and strapped himself in.

A metal strong-box containing flasks of purified water and soy protein cakes sat behind the rear seats in a storage locker. Along with a pair of shotguns and two boxes of shells. He hoped it wouldn't come to that. He'd already seen such a lot of violence since he left the Dome, but something told him it was far from the last. He existed in a new world now. A world with new rules: kill or be killed, apparently.

Gabe took the pilot's seat. Enna peered in from the other side, handed Gabe a HackSlate, and patted him on the knee.

Gabe winked at her before closing the gull-wing door with a satisfying clunk. Flicking switches and gesturing on the HackSlate, Gabe started the Jaguar on its ascent up the tunnel. The tunnel's sides were smooth, as if made of glass, and lit either side by a dotted strip of white light, which soon blurred to a continuous line as they picked up speed. Gerry closed his eyes tight and gripped the edge of the bench seat as his stomach cramped and became heavy with the G-force. Every muscle tensed against the upward motion, until they breached the open top of the tunnel and hovered over the ground.

Stars blinked and then blurred as Gabe tipped the front of the Jaguar downwards and activated the main jets, sending the vehicle forward with great speed. Looking out of the window, Gerry watched the building-top lights of GeoCity-1 shrink. He could just make out black dots scuttle between buildings.

"That feels better," Petal said.

"What does?"

"Leaving that hell hole behind. Thanks, by the way. For getting me to Enna in time."

Words wouldn't come, so he just smiled back. So many questions came to mind, but he wasn't sure he wanted the answers. Did she know what she was? Did she know what he was? Was she happy being paired with him? The dynamics had changed, and he felt awkward asking her these questions with Gabe sitting up front. In such a short time, things had taken on a considerably different aspect. Already he felt like a veteran ready for a war. Gabe seemed to sense his thought process.

"Why don't ya's get some sleep? Enna's GPS data says we're at least four hours from the Meshwork node of Seca's last known activity. She says the chips contained some metadata generating from an old super-computer. Beyond the sludge is another settlement."

"I thought nothing survived the Cataclysm?"

"There's a few places out there, man."

"What do you know about Seca?" Gerry asked.

"Only what Enna has told me. Why d'ya ask?"

"No reason. Just wondering if on your travels, you'd heard the name before."

"Nah, man. As far as I know, he's just some crazed hacker. We'll see, I guess."

Gerry dropped the line of enquiry, satisfied that either Gabe was lying about knowing Seca, given that he used to work for him, or he really did lose his mind like Enna said. He hoped it was the latter, the consequences of the former only meant bad news, yet he couldn't shake the idea that Gabe was delivering him and Petal into a lion's den. Despite the anxiety, he closed his eyes and let the tiredness seep through his muscles.

Before sleep completely took him, he was aware of Petal holding his hand, and his dermal implant buzzed gently. She was sending him a message via their VPN. He couldn't make it out, so just squeezed her hand as if to confirm that he was there for her.

Chapter 13

The Jaguar rocked violently. Gerry woke with a start. Petal's face stared just centimetres from him and reflected his own wide-eyed panic at the rapid changing of direction.

"We're going down! They hacked our navigation." Gabriel wrestled with the controls but couldn't steer the Jaguar away from its descent towards a narrow valley carved between red, dusty, flat-topped mountains.

"Who's hacked us?" Petal shouted above the wind and whining engines.

"Hell if I know."

The sun was rising above the ridge, casting the chasm into a golden, scarlet glow.

Gerry accessed his VPN connection with Petal. He branched out through a secure port to the Jaguar, tried to monitor the data of the Jaguar's system, but was instantly crashed out with a high-pitched screech in his communicator.

Involuntarily snapping his head away, Gerry slid across the bench seat, but the strapping held him before he could smash into the window as the aircraft lurched to its side, banking hard and down into a tight twist.

The ground spun and raced towards him. Amongst the movement, he noticed a number of black spots lined up aside a brown, sludgelike river at the bottom of the valley. Next to the black spots, a series of dust devils swarmed up into the sky. Ahead of the dust trails were heavy, four- and six-wheeled vehicles not dissimilar to those driven by the Bachians. Only these were far less jerry-rigged.

"We're gonna crash, Gabe. Do something," Petal said, her eyes growing wider still as she took in the scene.

"It's useless. These damn things are on rails. It ain't responding." Gabe yanked at the yoke and flicked switches to no avail.

The Jaguar slowed its fall before landing on a wide patch of dirt next to the sludge river, which flowed on slow, fat currents.

Gerry breathed slowly and waited for his head to stop spinning. Outside, three flat-bed trucks approached, carrying groups of people shrouded in black cloth.

On the back of the middle truck, a flagpole rose three metres into the air. A red and yellow flag, tattered and dotted with holes, whipped behind in the warm air.

The flag-bearing truck pulled up right beside the Jaguar. One man, wearing a featureless chromed mask and carrying a HackSlate, stepped down and stood at Gabe's door. Three more people appeared: two men and a woman. They wore cloth half-masks over their mouths and stood behind their apparent leader.

The two men both carried a pair of pistols, while the woman was armed with a long-barrelled rifle and scopes. She tapped the side of the gun, and a monopod extended to strike the dusty ground. She bent at the rifle and aimed it at Gerry.

Chrome Mask gestured on the HackSlate. The gull-wing doors of the Jaguar opened, and he beckoned them out.

"Get out. The vehicle's ours now."

"What the hell is this, Gabe?" Gerry asked, not moving. Scared to stay where he was, and scared to go out into the unknown.

"Hell knows. I ain't ever been this way before! Probably just survivors looking for resources."

They seemed far too professional for simple looters. The denizens of GeoCity-1 were far rougher than this lot, and they had the relative safety of their town. Out here, beyond the sludge, there was reputed to be nothing—not since the Cataclysm, anyway.

Chrome Mask turned to the woman with the heavy rifle and flicked his thumb towards the Jaguar. Before any of them had time to react, a shell scraped across the top of the aircraft, leaving a wide gash in the surface. The crack echoed around the valley, deafening them all. Gerry's ears rang with a metallic shriek.

Gabe shifted across and jumped down from the Jaguar. He raised his hand and helped Petal down before Gerry followed.

The woman looked up at him, sneered, and bent back down below the scopes. Her finger moved to the trigger. Chrome Mask's hand rose. Gerry's heart thudded out a tempo as if counting down. He closed his eyes, fully expecting to be blasted to pieces. But a hand grabbed his shoulder and pulled him towards one of the trucks. He was placed next to Gabe and Petal on a bench. Surrounding them, more of the same black-cloth, half-masked people sat staring, not saying a word. The truck belched into life, sending a plume of black smoke into the warm morning air, and jolted off down the valley.

Gerry turned to Petal. "So much for Enna's plan, then."

"Plans never mean anything, Gez. We'll sort it out," Petal said.

Gerry then turned to the nearest person in black. "Who the hell are you people? Can you speak? What do you want with us?"

No answer.

Behind him, the Jaguar's engines roared to life, and the aircraft flew ahead of them.

The truck trundled down the valley, following the path of the Jaguar. After a few kilometres, they had rounded the mountain completely, and the river grew wide and shallow. Brown sludge lapped slowly at rocks at the river's edge. Beyond the river a great canyon yawned open, and ahead of them a dirt road led to a city—an old city, perhaps even a dead one.

A series of high-rise buildings leant over as if they were about to fall. Their sides were charred and gouged by something explosive. Wire mesh sprang out of the concrete at obtuse angles like petrified spiders' webs. Rusted claws of rebar fingers reached for the sky.

Tattered signs, with words long-since abraded by the desert winds, hung from bent posts, creating a tunnel, which led to a previously wealthy city district. Buildings that would have once been aspiring glass monuments stood like metal skeletons next to older, more basic concrete constructs.

They travelled down what Gerry thought of as a high street. Smoke rose in a single column. The two trucks ahead of them stopped in front of an old, grand building. Their truck approached behind before stopping. Chrome Mask got out of the cabin. He pointed at Gerry. "You three stay where you are." He then beckoned his people to follow him into the building, and they were left alone in the back of the truck.

The place was quiet, like all places Gerry suspected were after such devastation: the quiet of the dead. He stood, looked around, and thought about running, when a series of green dots appeared at his feet. Looking up, he traced the laser beams—illuminated by the rakish angle of the sun and the dusty particulate in the air—to a series of five shadows in the windows of a tall burnt-out building.

"Wouldn't be that easy, Gez," Petal said with a shrug.

"What now, then?"

"Y'aint gonna do nothin' with them on ya. Just chill, man. They'd have killed us if they didn't want us for something. Sit down. Rest. It'll all shake out in the end."

"Do you know what's happening here?" Gerry said, wondering why Gabe was so calm about it all.

Gabe's eyebrows knitted together with incredulity. "What ya suggestin' here, man? Ya think I'd plan this— whatever this is?"

A gunshot silenced them.

Chrome Mask approached the rear of the vehicle and spoke, his voice muffled but still understandable.

"Get off the truck, and follow me. Slowly."

Together they did as they were told. Like a ridiculous superstition, Gerry tried not to step on the dancing green dots. As if touching one would bring down a bullet.

He jumped off the back of the truck and looked at Chrome Mask close up. Inside those dark eyeholes he saw a bright blue eye, staring, unblinking. The man reached up and slowly removed his mask.

When he raised his head, Gerry gasped.

One eye had rotted out. In its place just a scabbed, black sore sat, seeping a thick pus. Thick folds of skin twisted by burns covered his face. His lips turned up, creating a permanent sneer. Blackened nubs lined rotten gums, and a swollen tongue sat limply inside his mouth. Gerry looked away, unable to bear the sight.

"Who are you? What do you want with us?" Gerry asked.

The man replaced his mask, and his voice, deep and gravelly, laced with pain, spoke. "Where were you going?"

Gerry looked to Gabe, then to Petal for some guidance. None was coming. They looked as baffled at this man as Gerry felt. He tried to think of a convincing lie, but where else was there to go? He couldn't exactly say they were out for a spot of shopping or a trip to the park. Though clearly, there were more places out here in the supposed Abandoned Lands than anyone had let on previously. Or the Family had let on. How many more lies had they told the population? How many more places were hidden from those in City Earth? Was the Cataclysm not as all-encompassing as they were told?

Gerry sighed, feeling let down by the lack of support from Gabe and Petal.

"To a settlement is all. Just trying to get by, you know? Like the rest of you."

"You're lying," the man said. "I'll ask you again. This time, if you don't tell me the truth, I'll have all three of you shot."

"Hey," Gabe said. "Calm the hell down. There ain't no need for any of this."

"We're just hackers," Petal said. "Looking for work. We're on our way to a job. Some small place up by the Russian border. Nothing special."

Chrome Mask shook his head, and a rattling laugh came wetly from his throat. "Just because I'm not whole like you, you think I'm stupid?"

"No, no, not at all," Gerry said, giving Petal a glare. "We didn't mean—"

"Let me put you all out of your misery," the man said, standing back.

"No!" Gerry said, reaching out for him. "Please—"

"I meant," the man said, "I know where you were going. You don't have to come up with these ridiculous stories. No need for lies. I know more than you realise. We've been tracking your communications for the last few hours."

"You hacked us?" Gabe said.

Chrome Mask squinted with a smile. "Yeah. We're not without skills out here. How do you think we've survived this long?"

"So what now?" Gerry asked. "What is it you want with us?"

"I know where it is."

Petal stepped forward and bent her head slightly. "Where what is?"

"The node you seek. And I also know who usually accesses it. And now I'm left wondering whether you work for him—or if not, what your intentions are. I see your friend here is different to… everyone." He pointed a gloved finger at Gerry. "Your code is strange."

Gerry accessed his dermal implant, realised he was being scanned, and shut it down. Whoever this person was, they were an adept hacker. Gerry didn't even notice he'd got in. And now that familiar feeling of violation was back.

"I'm just a guy. Look, you've got our vehicle, why don't you just let us go? Maybe tell us where this Meshwork node is, and we can be on our way?"

"Yeah, man, we ain't lookin' to do no harm out here. Ya seem to have got ya 'selves organised. Ya don't need to be messin' with us." Gerry noticed Gabe lean hard on his right boot heel, priming his weapon. Gerry didn't want that, didn't want that in the slightest. As quick as Gabe was, Gerry doubted he'd be quick enough for the snipers. And as Gerry thought that, he saw the green laser dot creep its way across the ground, up Gabe's leg, past his chest, to where it rested on his forehead.

"Don't be a hero, old man," Chrome Mask said. "I'll do you three a deal. I'll take you to the node if you agree to do something for me in return."

"What do you want?" Petal asked. "You want to hire us for a job?"

"Software," he replied. "A self-executing, viral payload. You see, you might think of us as survivors, but really, we're victims. A plague has eaten most of my people, and I'd like to get the vaccine. Only the ones who created it have kept it to themselves and don't much feel like sharing with us Upsiders. And we can't do too much about it, being personae non gratae and stuck out here on the sludge borders. But you." Chrome Mask jabbed a finger into Gerry's chest. "You, my odd fellow, with your shifting, mutating code, you're different enough that I believe you could get passed their security. Deliver my program."

"Who exactly are you referring to?" Gerry asked as Petal gripped his hand.

"Seca and his little group of psychopaths. I'm assuming that's why you want the node, huh? He's been getting a little frisky on the Meshwork with his artificial evils lately. The node you seek has direct access to City Earth—I'm sure you know that by now. The Family don't know about it, though. Old Seca piggybacked their network while they were still building that Dome. He's clever. Insane, but clever."

"You called yourself an Upsider. What do you mean? What exactly is this place? What happened?"

"Ah, that's the question right there… what's your name?"

"Gerry. Yours?"

"You can call me Len. See, everyone refers to it as the Cataclysm. That's what the Family teaches all you Dome people. They're kind of being honest, but as with everything they do, it's not the whole of the truth. Look, I don't mean to freak you people out, but you've got to understand how tough it is outside of the Dome."

Gabe and Petal snorted. "You don't need to tell us," Petal said. "We've been out long enough to know all that. The only thing that's freaking me out is those damned scopes twitching about us. Wanna call them off?"

"They'll stay for the time being. Trust is a two-way

street, and I only travel one way."

Gerry looked him square in the eye. "If we can help you, then we will, but you need to give us some slack first. Show us the node." He just wanted to find the damn thing and get back to the Dome. Since leaving the City, he'd not felt right, as if he was constantly swimming against an ever-stronger tide, and frankly he was sick of it and fast running out of patience.

"Fine," the man said. "But any one of you takes a step out of line and your brains will be but fragments on the wind. Do you understand?"

They all nodded. Gabe gripped Petal's arm and gave Chrome Mask a wide grin.

Len gestured a single finger across his slate in a circular motion, and the green dots winked out of existence. Gerry looked up. Saw nothing in the windows.

Across the street, under a tattered canopy, a partially shattered glass door opened.

"Come on, then. Meet Omega, the node you seek."

***

Len opened the door and stood aside to let Gabe, Petal, and Gerry through. He led them through an old hotel lobby, its floor tarnished and charred, its wallpaper diseased with smoke damage, and its light fixtures melting as if exposed to extreme temperatures.

It was cool inside. Quiet too. Like a mausoleum. Gerry had only ever been in one: his parents'. Though that was much smaller—just big enough for two sarcophagi.

A tingling in the back of Gerry's head sent a shudder

down his spine as if he'd just been plugged into a power source. His thoughts became lighter. The slow, heavy thoughts of his non-AIA brain quickened, and he started to feel like his old self again. There was something else. The only way he could think of it was a permanently morphing fog surrounding him, almost as if it were reaching out towards him.

They quickly ascended a spiral staircase, dodging broken stairs and gaping holes as they kept up with Len's urgent strides. He loped like a great dog.

Two more black-clothed people stood beside the entrance to a hallway. Both leaned against the wall wearily, their guns hanging by the sides. They nodded curtly as Len passed them.

"Here. Number 24."

Len entered a code on the keypad, and the door creaked open. "Go inside."

The hairs on the back of Gerry's arms rippled—both from the cold and something more primal. One does not simply enter an unknown room in a strange hotel without the lizard-brain amygdala kicking out its survival signals.

The place stank of steam and mould.

Within the gloom, a bright, blue neon light glowed from behind a paper screen. In front, and sitting opposite each other on tattered sofas, were three more people wearing the same black cloth outfit and face masks. Gerry unconsciously held his breath as he walked in, wondering if the masks were needed to breathe properly in this steam, which now he was fully enveloped within and felt cold and wet.

He swallowed, breathing slowly through his nostrils.

Gabe and Petal followed him inside.

"I recognise this," Petal whispered to Gerry. "It's just like Old Grey's room. Keeps the CPUs cool."

"Is it safe to breathe in 'ere?" Gabe said, approaching one of the men on the sofas.

The figure didn't answer, didn't move. Even when Gabe reached out to grab the man, he just sat there. Gabe's hand went right through it, causing ripples of holographic pixels to flow around his hand.

"Please excuse my rudeness. These images won't hurt you. I just like their company." Len closed the door behind him and approached the paper screen as the hologram peeled away and morphed into another figure standing by a partially curtained window.

"It also doesn't hurt to have some figures walking about, just in case, you know?"

"In case of what?" Gabe said, frowning. "What are you so scared of?"

"Who. Not what. The Undersiders, of course. They want this."

He pulled the screen back and revealed a matte black box as big as a wardrobe. A multitude of wires wormed out from its rear and trailed across the hotel room's floor.

"It's the node," Gerry said as he rushed forward to it. He touched his hand against its thrumming chassis. The weird tingling sensation in his head and spine matched rhythms with the node, like two opposing tides becoming one, waves growing larger and faster. Sickness overcame him, and he fell to his knees.

"Gez, what's wrong?" Petal placed a cool hand on the back of his neck. "You're burning…"

Gerry swallowed, kept his eyes closed, tried to ride out the sick feeling. And as quick as it came upon him, it went away, leaving him feeling as if he'd been shocked by a stun-baton again. The holograms had risen from their seated position and now formed a protective circle around the node.

They stared silently with an implied malevolence like sleeping snakes.

"What's so special about this computer?" Gerry asked.

"I take it you've heard of Old Grey?" Len responded as he stepped forward.

"Are you saying this is the same model? An old-school AI?"

Len shook his head. "No, this has no intelligence that I can find, and yet…" He trailed off, apparently unsure of how to explain.

"Yet what?" Gerry urged him to continue.

"And yet, Seca has killed many of us Upsiders for it. It's the backbone of the entire Meshwork. His main access into City Earth. Without it, he would be severely crippled. It's his launchpad."

"And you let him access it freely?" Gerry stood, shaking his head with disbelief. "Why don't you just switch it off and prevent Seca from accessing it?"

"Don't you think I've tried?"

Gerry exhaled hard. "How can he access it without power?"

"Look." Len walked Gerry to the rear of the machine. "There is no power supply. You can't switch it on or off. It cannot be killed with EMP like what killed every other computer on the planet during the Cataclysm. It generates its own source somehow. Probably some kind of mega fuel cell or reactor. It created and maintains the Meshwork, but when you log in—which it allows freely—there's no AI in there, or at least none that I can find. Just an old pre-Cataclysm operating system from AppSoft.

"The damn thing is indestructible. And I make it my mission to keep it out of Seca's hands as much as possible. He still has remote access occasionally, but I've found that if I keep it moving, it causes him problems."

"Will you let me access it? To find Seca's location."

Len dropped his shoulders and breathed in. Considered.

Across the room, standing in front of the windows, Gabe circled one of the holograms, poked at it, and made its form shimmer. Other than that odd effect, there was no way of telling they weren't corporeal meat bodies. Still, Gerry wondered just how much of a defence they could be. Not being solid makes it somewhat difficult to wield a weapon or stop someone.

"Yes, but you must do something for me in return. The payload. I need you to install it in Seca's network. None of my hackers are capable of bypassing his security. But you're different… there's something about you. Something I think will help you crack his firewalls."

"What does it do?"

"It'll crack the security on the main compound where he keeps his vaccines and food resources. It'll hopefully shut down most of the servers that control the drones, cameras and locks. Once that has been bypassed, I'll have a couple of my people on standby to break in and get the resources we need."

Gabe turned away from the hologram and regarded Len with a pointing finger. "Look, man, ya could be setting us up with some dodgy bioSoft. How do we know it ain't gonna fry our brains? I've been on the wrong end of some shifty viruses in the past, and let me tell ya now, I ain't having none of that again."

The man took off his mask, exposing the mutated face and bloated tongue. Gerry wanted to look away from the sight of Len's disfigured lips twisting awkwardly as he spoke.

"Take a good look. This is the work of Seca and his buddies at the Family."

"His buddies? He's one of the Family?" Gerry asked, stunned.

"Yes. They instigated the Cataclysm. Poisoned the land and made all our parents freaks giving birth to more freaks, until all the interbreeding created people like me. People made to live Upside, scratching for survival among the dust." Len's face sneered with hatred as he worked up into a rage.

"All the while he and his people retreated to an underground city safe from the bombs and the poisons. For decades he's lived there, rebuilding himself, living luxuriously while everyone on the surface fights each other for safe territory and resources. And now his ego has grown too big!

"He wants revenge for being left behind by the Family as their experiment got out of hand and they built a Dome for their precious offspring. But what about us? What about our children that no longer live beyond a few weeks before their mutated genes kill them or twist them into hideous shapes? Who's going to look after us? It's all right for you Dome people living a life of complete safety and privilege as the Family's playthings. All your wants and needs are taken care of while the rest of us are forsaken."

Gerry tried to interject, ask some questions. The details were too much, too fast. But Len was frothing at the mouth as he continued his tirade.

"And now he wants to bring a war to us again. As if we haven't suffered enough! No, I can't stand idly by and watch us die out. All there will be left is AI 'borgs and robots. No more humans. Do you understand? No more humans! You take my payload and release it in his network. Then we'll see who'll survive a Cataclysm once we mount an offensive!"

"Dude, just chill. We'll do it," Petal said.

Gerry spun round. Petal stared back at him as if to say 'trust me'.

Gabe nodded at Gerry. He had no option but to agree. He wanted to just get this done as quickly as possible so that he could run all the ramifications through his head. Despite his newly active and faster working brain, it was still too much of an info dump to understand what was really being said.

Len reached into his jacket pocket, took out a DigiCard and a piece of paper, and handed them to Gabe. "When you get to Darkhan, look for an alehouse called 'The Blighty'. It'll be safe for you if you show them that piece of paper. They'll know what it is and what you need to do. The landlady will give you access to a secure node. Beyond that, you're on your own."

Len replaced his mask, turned his back, and approached

the door. As he walked out, he turned and regarded Gerry. "She's all yours. You've got five minutes. Don't get distracted when you're inside. Get in and get out. I don't want your Helix signature floating about on my nodes."

With that he closed the door and left them alone—apart from the hologram guards, who now split into multiple copies of themselves until there were six standing in a ring around the computer and Gerry. Petal and Gabe made to move into the circle with Gerry, but as they moved towards the holograms, a piercing green line of laser light created a ringed barrier. Petal moved closer until the beam touched her leather jacket, burning it instantly.

"What the hell?" Petal said.

The holograms turned in unison. Their eyes glowed.

"Be quick, man," Gabe said, backing off and dragging Petal away.

Gerry swallowed, approached what he thought was the front of the machine, and touched his hand to the warm chassis. Unsure of what to do, he turned to ask Gabe or Petal for some guidance when a stabbing pain shot through his brain, switched off his vision, and conjured an image of an old-fashioned computer screen in his mind. A pair of folder icons sat on the right-hand side of a dull blue-grey background. He mentally requested the opening of the one marked 'logs', and as he thought it, a pointer graphic moved across the screen, clicked the folder, and a set of files sprang open, arranged in date order. He opened the most recent and read the contents. A single line stuck out like a beacon:

—Darkhan:SIP:800:9220:892—D-185-%SECA—

It was a location registration with the same ID number

as the file on Old Grey.

That's it. Seca's location.

Gerry committed the numbers to memory and converted them to map points. He closed the file and the folder and requested a log-out. The computer disconnected him, and he found himself on his back, looking up at the glowing eyes of the hologram guards.

"Time's up," one of them said before its eyes glowed even brighter.

How could that have been five minutes? It felt like split seconds. Where had the time gone? And more worryingly: what had he, or the server, been doing during that time? He shook his head and backed away from the guards until he rejoined Gabe and Petal.

"Got it?" Gabe asked.

"Yeah, I got a lead on his location."

Chapter 14

The sun blazed like a beacon of hope high above them as their truck, kindly offered to them by Len, for three thousand bins, trundled across the black, scorched earth towards the city of Darkhan.

They were heading for a small district on the outskirts: a place the Upsiders had made their own. Len had dealt with this other group a number of times and developed a solid and trustworthy relationship with them, which enabled him to trade resources and, more importantly, get information on Seca and his group's movements and plans.

It was from that location they would be able to infiltrate Darkhan's tightly controlled security and gain access to a storage unit that contained the vaccines. Or at least, that was the plan. Len didn't give them much hope of breaching Seca's security after so many before them had failed. But Len knew Gerry was different somehow and entrusted him with a slither of hope.

Petal snored like a kitten next to Gerry in the front of the vehicle. He sighed quietly as Gabe piloted their way around craters big enough to swallow them whole. The ground was dry and cracked. Small patches of soy plants established themselves in pockets of fertile soil.

Nothing grew in the craters made from bombs, the various chemicals and heavy metals poisoning the land for many generations. The same poison that had mutated Len's people and their children.

The odd tingling sensation that first started back in Len's hideout remained, buzzing persistently like a mosquito with the scent of blood. Gerry sighed. It was a small price to pay for the increased cognitive performance. It was like someone had taken him from a grubby alley and got him cleaned up. Washed away layers of grime so that he felt fresh and rejuvenated.

With a slight return to his usual performance, he pondered on the nature of the hologram defence system Len had set up, and of the transcendents Enna was keen on building. It seemed that here, outside the Dome, humanity was not only struggling with the lack of resources—and the threat of a great and powerful enemy in the Family— but also the very core of what it means to be human. Did these holograms and transcendents have awareness of themselves? Did they know they were just constructs, or had their makers imbued them with a sense of self, a sense of life?

Petal shifted against him, yawned, and went back to snoring.

What was she exactly? She clearly had self-awareness and appeared human in every way...

Gerry admonished himself for glaring at her. She was something entirely other, yet so close to him. He felt she was the only one that could possibly understand what he was, what he could do. Given how few humans there were out here, he was thankful that Gabe and Petal had found him.

If Seca had his way, the Family, and by extension the Dome, would fall, and the world would be plunged back into a crippling war. Perhaps even the last war, and that would end the hope of those that managed to survive. A world of robots and transcendents living without humans chilled his bones.

The sight of a rising column of black smoke brought Gerry out of his musings.

"We got company. Best get ya weapon ready, man. Just in case," Gabe said.

Gerry was beginning to like the feel of the gun in his hands, the cold steel reassuring in its honesty. Pull the trigger and it goes bang. It was solid, simple, and final.

"Crap! How long was I out?" Petal asked as she lifted her goggles and rubbed her eyes with a balled fist.

"Coupl'a hours," Gabe said. "Look smart, girl, we're approaching Len's contact."

As they continued to weave in and out of the craters, a number of buildings appeared on the horizon: skyscrapers and many others in all kinds of sizes and shapes stood in the fog like grey fungi. Looked like it was once a wealthy zone, though one of the towers had its head blown off. Its innards lay hanging out of the architectural wound like a person's guts. One of the others looked similar to the buildings back at Len's. A hotel. Though like the others, it too cut a sad image with its windows boarded up with scrap metal and fragments of wood.

"Must have been a hard war," Gerry said. "The destruction is immense."

"Why d'ya think it was called the Cataclysm, man? Sure

weren't because it was a small affair. We're talking about a war so destructive almost the entire planet was wiped out. Notice the lack of animals yet, man? Humans—and only a handful, really—is what's left."

"Was it nuclear?" Gerry asked, frustrated at everyone skirting the issue.

"Yeah man. It was nukes, lots of other stuff. Perhaps it was the Family that fried us all from their space station. Maybe it was bugs or germs and people panicked. Lots of people guessing, but no one really knows for sure. Once the bombs dropped, it all went to shit. Apart from the Family, that is. They know everything that went on."

Gerry turned to see Gabe gripping the steering wheel so hard his knuckle bones shone through his thinning skin. There was an intensity to his eyes too. Staring straight ahead, he didn't blink for what seemed like minutes. Just steered at the broken buildings ahead, occasionally twitching his mouth into a sneer as he mumbled about nukes, EMPs, and other cataclysmic occurrences.

"Are you okay, Gabe?"

He ignored Gerry, continuing to grumble as he pressed the throttle on the truck and sped towards their destination.

Petal tapped Gerry on the knee and then sent him a message on their VPN.

It said: *"Chill, Gez. Gabe gets funny about it all. Don't push him. It's a sore subject."*

Gerry returned: *"Okay."*

But still, it played on his mind. Gabe was a strange one for sure, and now Gerry was questioning his loyalties, and not for the first time in the last couple of days. He just hoped whatever was going through his mind would stay away long enough to find Seca and put an end to his plans.

They arrived at a pair of heavily armed, and hastily built, checkpoints. Nothing more than hunks of twisted metal and a stool, on which sat two humanoids—for Gerry wasn't certain who was and wasn't human these days. They cradled dull-black metal weapons, which looked like cannons with their massive barrels and simple construction.

Petal leaned out the window and smiled at one of the grime-encrusted guards. He lifted a pair of sunglasses, revealing pupil-less eyes. They gleamed bright white in the sun as they swivelled in their sockets. The brute lifted the cannon, resting its barrel on the edge of the makeshift checkpoint.

"State your purpose and ID," it grunted.

Petal pulled from her leather jacket the paper Len had given to them. She held it up to the guard and snatched it away as he tried to take it from her.

"You don't need to take it to read it. Your pal Len's assured us you'd allow us through." She stuck out her chin, full of defiance.

The guard's eyes turned to a sickly yellow, like days-old custard. From within that gooey mess a black thing, like a marble, came to the surface and widened until the eyes were black orbs. The guard moved his lips as he read the ID document and note from Len.

"Go a hundred metres down this road. When you see the flags for 'The Blighty', park up behind the building and give this to the doorman." The guard handed Petal a Digi-Card with two holes notched into its surface near the top.

He removed the barrel from the checkpoint and waved them through.

The Blighty turned out to be a British-themed pub, or so Gerry was informed. He'd never seen such a thing, but warmed to it instantly. It had a homely feel with its soft cushion booths and dark wood tables. The bar ran the length of the room and featured a number of beer taps with various crests and icons signifying a range of ales. Pint glasses hung above the bar, and a barman with slicked-back hair wore a pristine white apron with 'The Blighty' emblazoned upon its surface in red thread.

The beer was not beer, a sign said, but a synthetic approximation. He was glad to have kept the water flask Enna had provided them. Despite the temptation, a synthetic version didn't appeal.

Much like The Spider's Byte, as soon as they breached the threshold, its patrons stopped everything to regard them in a tense silence. A particular woman caught Gerry's eye. She was leaning over the bar, sitting atop a wooden stool. She leant over to grab another refill from the optics behind the bar.

Gerry couldn't take his eyes off her as she slugged back a shot, slamming the glass on the bar and exhaling a loud whoop. She closed her eyes and tipped her head back, savouring the drink. When she opened her eyes, she caught Gerry in a fierce gaze.

"You. Come here." She pointed to Gerry. Her red nail polish gleamed in the orange light of the bar's low-level lamps. She hitched one leg over the other, stretching her leather miniskirt. She tapped the toe of a red stiletto boot against the wooden rung of the stool impatiently. Petal nudged Gerry in the ribs with an elbow.

"Go, Gez. That's our contact."

Gerry walked across the wooden floor towards her. Each step echoed with a thunderous clang, or at least it seemed that way with everyone glaring at him with a mixture of frowns and smirks.

When he got near, she grabbed the lapels of his leather duster and pulled him close. Her green eyes, like jewels, were just a few centimetres away. Her pupils expanded as she continued to analyse him.

"You're human," she said before letting him go. "I thought Len would find something... better." She sighed, pushing a lock of auburn hair away from her forehead.

"Are you an Upsider, like Len and his people?" Gerry asked, ignoring her obvious disappointment.

She turned her head away, focusing on the bottle and shot glasses on the bar. She poured another drink and slammed it back. "Something like that," she said, wiping her ruby-red lips with the back of her hand. "I'm Molly, and you, my little hacker, have work to do."

"How's this going to work?" Gerry asked.

"Simple. You come with me, do as your told, and see if you can hack Seca's security to deliver the payload before your brain explodes."

"Oh, is that all? There's me thinking it was going to be tricky."

"Yeah, you keep that confidence. You'll need it. Let's get to it, then." Molly stood, grabbed his hand, and led him to a door at the side of the bar. The various patrons had started to talk in hushed tones as he passed them. He noticed most of them had distorted faces like Len's.

Some had stunted limbs, misshapen arms and some that resembled flippers. A glimmer of hope shone in their eyes, adding to the responsibility that he felt growing heavily on his shoulders.

Before he let Molly take him through the door, he shot a look back at Gabe and Petal. Gabe grinned at him, urging him on. Petal's eyebrows knitted close, and her nostrils flared. Was she pissed off about something?

"Come," Molly ordered. She pulled his hand, dragging him through a beaded curtain and into a dark and dingy back room that stank of mould. Shrouds of thick red light illuminated an area at the back of the room. A leather sofa sat against one wall; a chair and a full-length mirror were opposite. Probably a two-way, he thought.

Molly pushed him roughly into the sofa and sat on the chair.

"Well?" Gerry asked, leaning forward. "What now?"

"Slip it in and drop your payload, Mr Techxorcist man," she said with a wicked smile. From inside her jacket, she took a beat-up HackSlate. An earlier model of the one Petal used. Its holographic display was partially broken, and the frame was dented and scratched.

"What happened to this?"

"It's the secure node," Molly said. "It got dropped a few times over the years as others tried to break Seca's security."

"What happened to them?"

"Better you don't know." She leant forward. Her face relaxed and became serious. "You have to remain focused. Don't let it get to you. If you get confused and let the fear get into your mind, you won't be able to crack the security."

"So this security that Seca has is an intelligent one? An AI?"

"Yeah… but it's messed up. It's not passive. It'll attack you as soon as you log in. Don't let it overwhelm you. You have to find a weakness, and when you do, drop Len's payload. The virus can only work from the inside. You understand?"

He gripped the HackSlate, took a deep breath, and tried to ignore the growing anxiety that was building within. He tried to calm his mind. Think back to all the jobs he'd completed at Cemprom when a rogue hacker had tried to get in. He took the DigiCard with Len's virus on it and installed it into the slot in the side of the slate. The software loaded within seconds, waiting for Gerry to download it into the right place.

A tingle of anxiety crawled up the back of his neck, making him shiver. Molly leant forward, resting her elbows on her knees. He caught himself distracted by her bare thighs beneath her miniskirt that had stretched upward.

"Eyes on the prize," Molly said with a smirk.

Gerry wasn't sure which prize she was referring to, but the bloom of embarrassment warmed his cheeks, and he looked away, trying to refocus. "What if the AI doesn't come to me?" Gerry asked. "How else can I deliver the payload if it doesn't make itself known?"

"Download it to the server node responsible for the security of the vaccine unit. But trust me. I doubt you'll have a free run of it. Although the slate will get you so far, all data on Seca's network is closely monitored."

Molly leaned back, crossed her legs, and lit a cigarette. The smoke filled the room, making the place hazy. It had a sweet aroma to it. Gerry's nostrils twitched as he breathed in the smoke. "What's that?" All cigarettes had been banned from the Dome. In fact, all non-medicinal drugs were banned. Which was no real problem as there wasn't anyone with the resources to manufacture recreational drugs.

"Just a little relaxant," Molly said, holding the cigarette between her forefinger and index finger so that it pointed away from her. She cut a cool figure sitting there shrouded in smoke. "I find it helps with these kind of things. Helps focus the mind."

A tickling cough played at the back of Gerry's throat, but he could feel himself become numb. His heart rate slowed, and his mind stopped whirling with anxiety.

"Just let it take you away," Molly said. Her voice was low and seductive. He wasn't sure if that was just her or the effects of the drugs, but he nodded, listened to her voice, and concentrated on his breathing. Once in the mindset, he connected to the HackSlate with his dermal implant.

"Are you ready?" Molly said.

"Yes."

"Okay. Once you log in, the HackSlate has a directory with the network address of the vaccine storage unit. The AI, however, is stored somewhere else. Don't worry about that. It'll come to you. Just get past it and locate the security node's exact address. The payload needs to know that to be fully functional. You'll see how it works when you activate it. It's super simple. The trick is surviving the AI."

Molly's form dissolved as the interface from the slate took over his optical nerve. A familiar sense of connection came in the form of a series of buzzes. His vision and perception went dark. A second later a gridlike interface filled his vision. Each square of the grid represented a program.

Following Molly's advice, he activated a directory on the interface and read the file within. It gave him the rough network address of the vaccine storage unit. The physical grid location showed it was situated within the centre of Darkhan city, some twenty kilometres from his current position. That physical distance, however, was of little consequence. The network allowed him to reach the node that managed the security of the vaccine unit with a few thoughts of his mind.

He began to analyse the flow of data on the network as it passed through the HackSlate. That was one of the device's main uses: it would spoof itself as a computer on the network and divert traffic through its processor, where the user could alter the data to his or her desire.

In Gerry's case, he wanted to hack into the security server and deliver the software virus Len had created. A strategy was starting to form.

The data that he analysed was various instructions from the vaccine unit to the security server and back again. At first he thought he'd have a free run at it and would be able to drop the payload. Optimism was a cruel mistress, though.

The AI charged with keeping the vaccines safe and secure had shut off the flow of data and zeroed in on Gerry as his mind delved deeper into the flow of bits.

A sensation like being electrocuted surrounded his head. His first instinct was to disconnect from the Hack-

Slate, but his retreat was blocked, and he fell further into the network, compelled by the massive code base of the security system. Although he wasn't in a VR world, the AI appeared to be similar to the one he saw back at Enna's place: tentacular within its system of multifunctioning programs, all branching out from a central, intelligent body.

With a foreboding sense of horror, Gerry realised that the code his brain was developing to counteract the AI was actually feeding into it. The electrical buzzing in his mind increased as he put more and more of himself into keeping up with the attacks. The AI pumped gigabytes of data a second through the system to Gerry, overloading his neural capacity to cope with the flood of information. It was like someone had attached audio and video feeds directly to his ventral pathways in the parietal lobe—the part of the brain responsible for integrating information from the different senses in order to create a picture of the world.

Sweat poured from his forehead. His heart rate beat faster than he thought was even possible. Code spun out of his mind chaotically as he panicked in trying to stem the flow from the AI.

He wanted to shout out or scream, but that part of the brain remained unavailable. All resources were busy in dealing with this attack. From somewhere far out of his cognition he heard Molly's voice.

"Calm down, Gerry. Focus on the AI's central core. Ignore the other programs. They're decoys."

Her voice came to him in snatches, and it took a few seconds to fully comprehend the words. But eventually they built up a picture in his mind of what to do.

One of the anti-hacking programs from the AI attempted to attack his temporal lobe, the area of the brain that managed perception, learning, and memory. Gerry went on the counter-attack. He couldn't afford for that part to be damaged. It was the core of everything he was able to do. Without the ability to form memories or learn, he'd be nothing more than a dumb unit like one of the NearlyMen.

Focusing all his energies on a single spearlike program, he constructed a complicated process using some of the ideas he learned from the Helix++ book: A set of algorithms that mutated at an exponential rate.

Dropping the software program into the flow of traffic between him and his attacker, Gerry let his mind follow behind, using the software as a kind of mine sweeper. Such was its size and increasing nature, it started to overwhelm the intelligent code and made it use more of its own resources to cope with Gerry's counter-attack.

One by one, the tentacular applications that made Gerry's mind buzz like a transformer dropped away as their code fragmented under his attack.

"You're close, Gerry! Keep going," Molly's voice called out from beyond a veil of darkness. It gave him hope, and he plunged further into the computer system, letting more of himself become binary, all the time pushing his countermeasure forward.

He knew he was gaining ground. The security program had uninstalled all but one of its processes in order to battle Gerry's software tool and had retreated to its own server where, presumably, it had its own firewalls to protect it.

That was an interesting thought right there: the AI was concerned with self-preservation. If it did retreat completely, it would give Gerry a clear route to the computer responsible for the security system on the vaccine storage unit.

Energised and feeling the adrenaline course through his body, Gerry put one last effort into his attack, forcing the ever-growing program ahead of him as his consciousness became one with the network.

The AI appeared to scream and shrink as Gerry thrust out with his mind. He chased the intelligent software through the flows of data. Ahead, he could sense a much larger network of computers. A specific node was open and waiting.

Sensing it was a trap, Gerry eased off as the AI pulled away into the node. A firewall slammed shut, deleting his attack program, leaving Gerry unprotected. But more importantly, the AI was securely on the other side. He grabbed the opportunity. Forgetting about the AI, he took the risk of turning his metaphorical back on it and raced his mind through the connections of computers until he found the vaccine unit's node.

"Now or never," he thought as he dropped in Len's payload virus.

It unfolded immediately, creating a storm of code cascading through the network like white, rushing waters breaching a dam. It caught Gerry in the wake, frying his brain with an impossible level of feedback. He just caught sight of the vaccine node crashing under the effects of the payload before his vision turned to black.

***

A physical jolt that made his body spasm uncontrollably ripped through him like a flash of lightning. The Hack-Slate fell to the floor in a pool of blood. A pair of hands were on his head and another on his ankles.

"What the hell? What happened? Where…" He tried to speak, but the words jumped from his throat like rats from a sinking ship. The room spun. He felt like a hot poker had been forced into his brain stem. Lava flowed up and down his spinal column.

"Hold on, man," said a voice. He couldn't tell if it was male or female, the words distorted. Pressure increased on his head and ankles when he felt bile rise in his throat. With a single convulsion, he arched his back, breaking the grip from the dark figures. He turned to his side and threw up on the floor.

A hand pressed gently against his back. Another brought a cloth to his face.

Once he got his breath back and wiped his face, the room stopped spinning. It was still smoky from earlier, and the air was still rich with that sweet aroma. He breathed it in, taking in great lungfuls, replenishing his body with oxygen. The drug, whatever it was, helped to reduce his heart rate and clear the burning sensation in his brain.

"You did it, Gez." Petal kneeled beside him. "That was incredible. I've never seen anything like it."

Sitting made a bright flare explode in his vision. It cleared shortly after Gabe, Petal, and Molly helped him to the sofa. He looked to the floor and saw the mess he had made.

"I've got to stop doing that," he said, pointing to the pool of vomit.

"Just your body's way of dealing with the trauma," Molly said. "I've seen worse. The last hacker who tried to get to the vaccines had his brain leak out of his ears. Yours, Gerry, seems in one piece."

As if confirming that his brains hadn't actually leaked out, he reached his hands to his head. The throbbing had started to clear. Presumably the calming effects of the drug. "That was fucked up," he said. "Worst experience of my life."

"But ya did it, man," Gabe said, grinning widely in the dark. "Ya delivered the payload."

"What now?" Gerry asked. "Are we done here?"

Petal sat next to him. "Yeah, you held up our end of the bargain. We can go."

"I don't think he's in any state," Molly said, putting an arm around Gerry. "I think he should stay here with me for a while."

Petal pushed her arm off Gerry's shoulder. "Get your mitts off him. He's done enough for you."

Molly backed away, raising her palms. "Easy, girl. I didn't mean anything by it."

"Yeah, well, he's been through a lot, is all."

"Hey," Gerry said. "I am still here, you know." He stood and waited for his balance to recalibrate. It felt like he was walking on ice for a moment. He reached out as he tipped forward. Gabe stopped him and held him up in a mirror image of their first meeting.

"Thanks, Gabe," Gerry said. With his help, he turned to

Molly. "There is one thing you can do for me, if you want."

"Sure, name it." Molly gave him a coquettish smile.

"Any chance of a drink? Something strong? I'm bloody parched after that."

"Sure thing, babe, come with me. Drinks are on the house for all of you today. It's the least we can do."

Chapter 15

Molly led the three of them through to the bar. A ripple of applause came from the various patrons. The news had clearly got out. Gerry blushed with the attention. Petal stood by his side and elbowed him gently in the ribs. "Look who's Mr Popular Guy today, eh?"

"I don't know about that," Gerry said. "I was just doing a job. It was Len's payload that did the heavy lifting. I just dropped it in."

"Sure, that's all you did. You're too modest, Gez. You kicked that thing's ass in a way I've never seen before. Man, that was freakin' awesome."

Gerry shrugged, returned Petal's infectious smile, and took his seat next to her in one of the plush, cushioned booths. Molly brought him a bowl of hot soup and a pint of purified water. After serving everyone, she slid in next to Gabe.

"Well, you lot," Molly said. "All us Upsiders owe you a debt of gratitude. That was spectacular."

"What happens now?" Petal said.

"We take over." A shadow stretched over the booth. The bar became silent. Gabe looked up, his face impassive. Gerry and Petal looked around and saw two masked figures in black standing by their booth. Each one carried a long rifle on their back and a number of weapons on their belts: knives, pistols, batons.

Gerry recognised the one who spoke. The woman who had fired at him when Len's people first brought the Jaguar down. She stared at Gerry as if analysing him for something. "You did well," she said. "I appreciate that. It couldn't have been easy, and you took a huge risk for us. I for one thought you wouldn't go through with it. But Len trusted you."

"Um, thanks," Gerry said. "I'm pleased I could help. What will you do now?"

"Ghanus and I," she pointed to the mute man standing beside her, rippling with muscles beneath his dark form-fitting clothes, "will storm the unit and recover the vaccines before Seca manages to reboot the security system. I just wanted to come back to thank you for giving us this opportunity. I'm afraid we don't have time to stay here and show our gratitude fully."

"I understand," Gerry said. "I hope you get the vaccines."

"We will. One way or another," the woman said. She held out her gloved hand to Gerry. "I'm Liza-Marie, by the way. It's a pleasure to meet you."

Gerry took her hand. "I'd say the same, but you shot at me." He gave her a quick smile to show he was joking, but she didn't react. She shook her head before releasing him and turned away with her compatriot.

"We have transport into Darkhan if you want to come with us," she said, stopping at the door. "And by transport, I mean the truck Len gave you. Sorry, but we had to commandeer it. Vehicular resources are scarce these days.

And Len didn't want to risk the Jaguar in the city. Too many drones floating about."

Gabe stood, incensed that they'd taken the truck. Gerry put a hand on his shoulder. "It's all right, Gabe. I'm ready to go. We can take this with us." He pointed to the soup.

"I'll box it up for you," Molly said. "You should go with them. You can't simply walk into Darkhan on your own."

Gerry thanked her, took the boxed soup and flasks of water, and with the others followed Liza-Marie and Ghanus to the truck. The journey into Darkhan would take about an hour, Ghanus said, as they set off towards the city. There was no small talk between them as Ghanus drove the truck through a labyrinth of tunnels and tight roads, snaking between ramshackle buildings and shanty dwellings.

Groups of mutated survivors huddled together in hovels and hastily made tents. They all just stared at them with their milky eyes as they drove further into the city.

Ghanus stopped the truck in a dark alley.

"This is your stop," he said, looking into the back of the truck where Gerry, Gabe, and Petal sat on the hard wooden bench. "Good luck with whatever you're trying to do."

And that was that. Gabe led them out of the rear of the truck, and a second later Ghanus drove off to leave them there in the middle of the city.

"Right," Gabe said. "We should probably go find Seca's compound while we're here. Ain't exactly a place for sight-seeing."

Gerry and Petal followed Gabe as he strode out into the city like some kind of aboriginal bushman.

***

Darkhan sprawled like a chaotic maze. It featured much of the same damage to the tall buildings as the last place. Dark streets melted between centuries-old architecture. Old stone museums stood proud and relatively damage-free next to crumbled glass and steel structures.

Rudimentary tents hung from the sides of office blocks and shopping centres. Their dirty brown material sagged in the middle. Probably to catch what little rain came. Gerry doubted it'd be safe to drink. But given the state of the people huddled under their makeshift roofs, he knew they were unlikely to be too concerned anymore. Their still-bright eyes shone out from blackened faces. Kids with lank hair chased each other through the makeshift shanty streets.

Occasionally, Gerry spotted groups of men and women carrying stun-batons, enforcing some inner-city law, taking things from the people at the lowest level. It sickened him to see humanity degenerate into such an abusive system. Given how few remained outside of the Dome, he'd have hoped they'd have helped each other instead of preying on the weak for scraps of food and clothing.

Gabe forced a way through a shambling horde of filthy Upsiders. Gerry and Petal followed behind. The dishevelled people stank of rotten vegetables and things too bitter and sweet to be anything other than days and weeks of encrusted body odour. Gerry gagged, pulling his shirt over his mouth and nose as he continued to push his way down the crowded street.

On either side of the street, blackened buildings rose into the sky. The sun was dipping down towards the horizon, casting long, raking shadows across the narrow street.

Now that Len's people were on their way to get their vaccines, he hoped these people could get better. Hacking coughs caused streams of blood to flow down the chins of a group of men and women stood around a small fire. Gerry noticed the lack of children, just as Len had intimated.

"Fresh meat, roasted only yesterday," shouted a street vendor from behind a column of steam. Gerry's guts turned with the smell. He was glad he had the ration packs. He couldn't live like these poor bastards.

"What the hell is that?" Gerry asked, pointing to the blackened 'meat' as they passed the vendor within his alcove made from the crumbled side of a building.

"Man, that stuff's riddled with hagworm," Gabe said. "Everything here is. It'll eat ya guts out right from inside ya." Gabe pushed on further into the crowd.

As Gerry followed, the buzzing in his head grew more insistent, like a bee trapped in a jar. Only every now and then, he'd get a flash of an image, of home, of his wife and kids, of his job. It was like memories were being found, dragged from dark, hidden corners. Maybe his brain was repairing itself after having most of his images wiped when he uninstalled his AIA. Perhaps they weren't stored with Mags after all.

"Gez, over here." Petal reached back, grabbed his hand, and pulled him through a thin slice between buildings. Daubed on one side was a set of numbers in barely visible paint. Gabe took a torch from his jacket and shined it on the markings. The numbers seemed to label the wall, as if it were a grid reference. Gerry ran his hand over the stone of the building. It was warm to the touch, despite being completely in shadow. A faint rumble travelled through his fingers.

"Seca's place must be close by. There's definitely a power source or something under here."

Petal took out her HackSlate and pulled up some notes. "Len said there were a number of entrances across the city. It's got to be around here somewhere." Using a partial map, she tapped and swiped her fingers across the 3D image of the buildings. "I'm getting Meshwork traffic signatures from further down here. I'll patch you in."

A flood of information flowed across his VPN, connecting him to something larger: the actual Meshwork. It wasn't via his dermal implant either. It was as if he was integrated directly.

In his mind he pictured the torrent of bits crash around him like a white-water river, and then he saw patterns. He did his trick of sorting data and soon built up a picture of the city and the flow of computer traffic. Like a bloodhound, he pushed his way in front of Petal and Gabe and began to lead them through alleyways and across abandoned parks, always moving towards the nexus of data. His heart pounded, and his lungs burned as he realised he was sprinting.

"Hold up, man!" Gabe shouted. Gerry shook his head, cleared his mind, and looked behind him. Gabe was helping Petal to catch up. She looked so frail now. Had he not noticed her deterioration over the last few days? Had she just grown weaker in these last few minutes?

He admonished himself for being so neglectful. Enna had wanted him to look out for her, and here he was, getting carried away, thinking only of himself—and his kids. He took a breath and waited for Gabe and Petal. Behind them, he spotted something black and sleek take off from the top of a tower and fly down towards them.

"Drone!" Gerry pointed behind them. "Hurry up." He looked around him. He was now in the open, standing in the middle of a great field of dead, brown plants. Spotted about the place, huddles of people, presumably dead or at least dying, lay like great stones. No real cover anywhere. They had to get across the field to the next sector of the city, to the nexus of data.

"I thought the payload grounded the drones?" Petal asked as she sprinted towards Gerry.

"It did. For a while," Gerry said. "Must have got them all back online."

Petal twisted her head to see the drone and stumbled. Gabe managed to catch her and helped make up the ground. Gerry dashed towards them, and propping Petal up with Gabe, they shuffled their way across the field, all the while stealing glances behind them as the black shape closed the gap.

A crash erupted across the sky, and a great sod of dirt exploded just a few metres to the side of them.

"Run for it," Petal screamed, pushing Gerry ahead of her as she and Gabe steered off in opposite directions.

The drone flew past them and over Gerry's head before sweeping round to face him. It was like a black swan. Sleek, but deadly. A laser point shone from its nose. It danced on the ground ahead of him as he continued to sprint, dashing in sharp angles in order to avoid it, but the beam tracked his every move, and then it found him, crawling up his arm and shining in his eye. The drone hummed as it recharged its cannon.

A particle beam the width of an adult's hand shone from a barrel beneath the drone's matte-black fuselage. It aimed right for Gerry's face. He twitched away at the last possible opportunity as the cannon fired a stream of charged ions into the ground beside him. The heat scorched the side of his face, making his skin fizzle and burn with spots of super-heated mud.

He lost his balance and tripped over a rock, crashing into the ground. Gabe and Petal shouted at him. Both voices came from different locations. His head spun and chest heaved as the drone approached and wound up its cannon once more.

Gerry rolled to his side, grabbed the gun from his waistband, and instinctively fired off two rounds. The first missed, but to his surprise, the second hit and knocked the drone off its current trajectory, sending it into a barrel roll. Taking advantage, he got to his feet and spotted both Gabe and Petal reaching the end of the field and entering the next district of closely built buildings.

Petal sent a message across their VPN. It just said: 'RUN!'

So he ran.

Every few steps the dread grew. He wanted to look behind himself, but daren't lose the time. The familiar whine of the drone's engines grew louder. He knew it was right behind him. He could smell the gas from the particle cannon. Petal waved frantically, urging him to sprint, but his legs were growing heavy, and a painful stitch made every breath feel like a stab in the heart.

Sweat dripped down his face to mix with the still-hot mud splatters.

He wiped a hand across his cheek to clear it and gritted his teeth for the final stretch.

The laser guide danced to the left of his feet. He counted for two seconds, listening to the cannon power up, and then dove to the right as soon as he heard the explosion. The bolt missed him—just. He turned to see the drone hover no more than twenty metres above him. It dipped, shone the laser on his chest, and wound its cannon up to speed.

Pain shot up his leg as he fell into a pothole. He tried to pull it free, but the pain and awkward angle prevented him from moving.

"Run, Gez. Get the hell out of there," Petal screamed. Her voice grew louder, and he knew she was running towards him.

"Stay back. Save yourself. Get to Seca's place."

Gerry aimed his gun and fired off two more shots. The third returned an empty click. Both shots clipped the side of the drone, but it soon corrected itself and floated down to just three metres above him. Gerry closed his eyes, convinced he was just seconds away from being blasted by an ion stream, when a voice spoke from a speaker within the craft.

"You're quite disappointing in the flesh, Mr Cardle. My little lure, my Architeuthis, found something talented in you, but maybe you're not as special as I first thought. I thought you'd do better than this. Maybe I overestimated your abilities after all. Well, I'm not one to look a gift horse in the mouth."

"Seca? You bastard, you utter—" Gerry frothed at the mouth and couldn't get his words out. The pain grew red hot in his leg as he pulled it free. Tears clouded his vision, and the whine of the cannon pressured his eardrums so that a low rumble encompassed his hearing.

Everything slowed down. His heart stopped racing, and his mind switched on. In front of him: the same flow of Meshwork computer traffic as before. The nexus lay just behind him beyond the fields, and there in the middle, flowing towards the drone, a thin stream of information. Packets of bits bouncing back and forth, carrying instructions and data.

The rumble increased in power, becoming a high whining noise. He knew it'd fire any second, but still he remained calm as he dove into the flow of information, probed at the packets of info, and traced their route back to the nexus. A node, no more than a small server amongst many, housed the AI that controlled the drone. Gerry ripped through its firewall with ease, crashed terabytes of junk information into every available port, and swamped the AI with as many processes as Gerry could handle. The flow of traffic to the drone decreased, then stopped as the AI ran out of resources to deal with Gerry's assault.

The drone still fired.

Chapter 16

The ion blast crashed into the ground off in the distance. Hands gripped Gerry's shoulders and heaved him out from his trapped position just as the drone crashed into the ground within a metre of his last position.

"Gez, you okay?" Petal stood over him, her goggles up and eyes full of concern. Her skin glowed with a sickly sweat. She was paler than ever and looked so frail. He looked around, convinced he imagined everything and had actually been hit by the cannon. But there she stood, leaning over him, her warm hand on his cheek. Her voice softened as their eyes met.

"Speak to me, Gez. Are you hurt?"

"Apart from a near heart attack, I think I've broken my ankle."

She brought her face close to his, but still their eyes locked onto each other. She wiped away the hot mud from his face. Her lips pouted with concern. They were so close to his face now...

"You're burned, Gez. It's okay. We can fix that."

She reached into her jacket and pulled out a syringe of NanoStem. Before he could protest, she jabbed his ankle and plunged it into his bloodstream. It instantly cooled the sprain and tingled as if he had pins and needles. "Try to keep your weight off it. The 'Stems will fix that bone right up."

She smiled at him then and turned her attentions to the drone. "How did it know we were here? I thought the payload was supposed to knock out his servers and stuff?"

Gerry didn't know, but Gabe's absence was telling. Ever since Enna had tasked Gerry with looking after Petal—though it seemed the other way around—he'd suspected there was something else going on with Gabe. Trust was now being called into question, which was never a good thing. It made decision-making almost impossible when a key member of that equation was unknown in his motivations.

"How did you do it?" Petal asked. "Did you hack it?"

"I'm not entirely sure. Panic set in, and the next minute I know I was in the network. I must have piggybacked the VPN and found myself in the Meshwork. Seca had an AI controlling the drone. What else has he got automated to such a level? The network is vast… I don't know how we—"

"We'll find a way, Gez. Come on. Gabe's waiting. He's found an access into the compound."

"Are you okay? You're not looking well. Do you have any more NanoStems for yourself?"

"Uh huh." She smiled again, but Gerry knew she was lying.

"Petal, tell me straight. What's happening to you? You used the last of the 'Stems on me, didn't you?"

"Look, I'm fine. I can do this. Just get a move on, yeah? We've got a job to do."

Just like that, the warmth had gone, the goggles came

down, and Petal was back to her mysterious self. How could he look after her if he didn't know what she needed? Enna should have given him more information. Hell, Petal should let him help her if Gabe wouldn't.

"Is it an addiction? To the 'Stems?"

"I said leave it, Gez."

"Or are you sick from containing the demons and AIs?"

Petal ignored him and walked off towards the edge of the field.

Resigning himself to not knowing, Gerry limped after her, his ankle numb to the pain as the NanoStems repaired the damage. Or killed the nerve endings. He wasn't entirely sure how they worked. And didn't care. He had a sniff of Seca and now wanted to finish him.

For good.

Using Petal's HackSlate, Gabe traced a route through the city until he arrived at a manhole covered by rags and detritus. "Down here. Can ya feel it?"

Gerry placed a hand on the metal cover and, like the building before, it had a warm vibration to it, like servers, and rows and rows of computing power. Instinctively he felt the sheer amount of processing that must be going on in the Underside.

Gabe lifted the cover and waited for Petal and Gerry to go down before climbing down and replacing the cover. A sickly green light shone from far below them, lighting their way down the metal-runged ladder. They must have descended for over a hundred metres by the time the light fully lit the corridor. It reminded Gerry of the submarines in films he'd watched as a kid. He couldn't remember much about them now, but the circular metal gangways felt familiar.

Myriad tubes of thick copper and fibre-optic cable ran down the sides of the tunnels. Like a raging river, information blasted through the network.

"We should turn off the VPN," Gerry whispered to Petal. "And your HackSlate. We can't afford to transmit anything down here. You too, Gabe."

They both nodded at him, switched off their slates, and Petal turned off their VPN.

Gerry noticed the lack of connection as his dermal implant switched off. Even the subtle red LED, put there by Gabe to 'assess his code' what seemed like decades ago, but which really was just a few days, blinked out. And yet, weirdly, he still felt connected to… something.

Was it the Meshwork? Or Seca's own network? Or maybe it was just a vestige of being connected to Petal via their VPN for so long. Nothing more than a phantom feeling amplified by the stress of the situation and the 'Stems doing their thing on his ankle.

The three of them followed the tunnels, Gerry giving direction as he seemed to feel his way around, sensing his way towards the hub of the network. In truth, it was just the vibrations in the metal tunnel; he went where it felt the strongest. Neither Gabe nor Petal felt it strongly enough to guide them. Gerry thought it was a case of him being fairly new to life outside the safe confines of the Dome and thus more sensitive. Petal and Gabe had been living off the grid for years, surrounded by their own personal computer networks. They were used to the hum and buzz of electricity, cooling fans, and processors.

"I hear voices up ahead. Wait." Gerry pulled up, turned,

and whispered. He swore to himself as he realised he hadn't reloaded his weapon. Petal silently extended her chrome spike from her inner arm and flattened her back against the tunnel as the echoing voices drew closer.

The green light from an exit just a few metres ahead wavered; then shadows appeared on the dull, metal floor. Gerry could hear the footsteps and the laughter real close.

Petal breathed into Gerry's ear, "After three…"

She counted to two, slithered past Gerry, and drew back her spike ready to attack, when two men in stealthy, dark grey and black armour turned into their tunnel. Before Petal had time to attack, Gerry felt something cold against his throat.

"Just stay still, man. Don't move…"

"Gabe! What the?"

Gabe pushed a sharp blade into Gerry's throat, holding him against the wall.

"Nice work, old man," one of the guards said as they crashed a stun-baton into Petal's face, sending her instantly to the floor in a heap.

"What have you done? Why?" Gerry couldn't understand. It was happening too fast.

Then it was his turn. The guard, wearing a sick smile, raised the baton and smashed Gerry across the temple, sending bolts of electricity through his brain, bringing the darkness in a rushing torrent.

Chapter 17

His body twitched beyond his control. Tiny currents activated his muscles in excruciating ways. The pain didn't stop—just changed form like an energy source. It started with cramps in his legs and arms, and then shooting pains up his spine. Then it was his heart and lungs receiving stabbing sensations. It felt like someone was pushing burning needles into his organs.

Despite his eyes being open, he couldn't make out anything through the blurry film of sweat and tears. Indistinct shapes hovered not far from his face, but all he could sense was pain.

He couldn't shout out. A gag had been tied tightly around his head, cutting into the corners of his mouth. His body jolted again. This time he felt the ice-cold tip of a metal rod touch the burned flesh on his face.

Close to his ear, he heard a laugh.

The voice seemed familiar, and then it spoke to him.

"You think this is pain? You think you're going to die eventually? You think this is torture? You're wrong."

It was the voice from the drone. It was—Seca.

The cold steel tip traced an arc across his cheek to his right eye. He held his breath until his lungs burned, but still the pain didn't come. Forcing himself against restraints that held him to a metal board, he thrashed uselessly. He knew it. Seca knew it. But still Gerry fought. Would fight until he had nothing left. Until, that is, Seca sent a bolt of electricity down the rod and into his eye, frying it instantly within its socket. His brain reeled back into his skull, horrified at the attack on one of its senses. He wished for unconsciousness, but something kept him awake and fully aware of what was happening.

Something switched on inside his mind. That insistent tingling he felt before increased and grew to a deafening buzz before completely shutting off, leaving a void in his consciousness.

Then a familiar voice inside his head spoke.

- *No new messages. Your newsreader app was cancelled three days ago. The City Earth Police Enforcement officially wants you. I'm regulating the work of the NanoStems. You have a lot of internal injuries, Gerry. The optical nerve to your right eye is beyond repair. I'm adjusting focusing and depth perception to monocular vision.*

At first, Gerry thought it was a dream. A drug-induced flight of fancy his subconscious decided to take him on in order to deal with the pain and the trauma. But no, he was awake, breathing through the gaps in the gag and his left eye blinking spasmodically to clear the salty film. That voice, inside his head, was well known to him. Magdalene—his AIA. But how?

Tentatively he reached out with his mind and sent her a number of basic instructions. She responded.

- *Your blood-sugar level is low, Gerry. You should find something to increase it. It will help the healing*, Mags said.

- Mags, how can you be working? I uninstalled you, Gerry replied.

- You can't uninstall me. I AM you. You somehow temporarily disabled me, but I found a way through.

- How? You are me? What do you mean? You're my AIA… installed as a kid like all the—

- No. We're different, Gerry. I was never installed. We were born as one. Made as one. While you ring-fenced me, I had time to look through our root files. The Family created us.

Gerry's mind folded in on itself as questions about his life, his birth, his mortality, and even his species crashed together like a supercollider. Was he even human? Was he a kind of cyborg? Is that what Enna was getting at? The data from these questions flashed by in nanoseconds, discounting theories and branching into hundreds of lines of inquiries. It made so much sense now. Explained how he could analyse data in the way he could and build algorithms that no one else could.

- Mags. We need to get off Seca's network. We're being watched.

-It's because of Seca's network that I was able to free myself. But we do need to remove ourselves from here. There's a multiple terabyte demon AI travelling about the network. It's heading for City Earth. It'll destroy everything. The one heading for the president was just a decoy, a lure. We need to get back to the Dome, to their internal systems.

- Can't we access a City Earth node from here? How's their defences?

- Assessing.

"Not so strong. Not so much fight after all. It never

ceases to surprise me how quickly your species gives up with the introduction of a little pain," Seca said as another bolt of electricity blasted into Gerry's nervous system. This time the attack was on his chest, and he bucked violently against his straps. He thought his spine would snap as his muscles involuntarily tensed towards the source of the pain. He bit down on the gag, refusing to give in, and retreated into his mind.

Gerry analysed the flow of data as Mags pinged a cloaked query through the Meshwork to the Dome's system. The request returned, bringing a log file with it: nothing. No firewall. It had been breached, leaving City Earth's systems wide open to attack.

- That must have been the work of Architeuthis or Jasper, Gerry said. *We need to repair the damage, get some kind of defence up. Can we access their defence servers?*

- We can piggyback the demon AI, but the tunnel through the Meshwork is littered with scanners. We'll be spotted. And City Earth's internal systems aren't on any network. They need direct access.

- How is the demon going to get in, then... Of course! Jasper! He's the inside man. Let me take a look at the AI.

- Patching.

Hot breath breezed across his ear. "I sense what you're doing, Gerry. Frantically trying to understand. Trying to find a way of stopping me. But just look at it. Look at my creation."

Mags and Gerry, now together as one, dropped their consciousness into the river of Meshwork traffic within Seca's network, and then Gerry saw it: Seca's AI. It was elegant: infinite loops within infinite loops of self-executing programmes. All wrapped up into a single intelligent, and utterly malicious, software demon. It was as if it were a living thing. Myriad subroutines managed resources while others processed wildly complex simulations. The sheer amount of data it was getting through was unlike anything Gerry had seen before. It sat within the Meshwork in its entirety like a black hole. Nothing escaped its gravity pull—including Gerry and Mags. Seca must have seen everything they had done since the day his lottery numbers came through.

This was it: the genesis, the nexus, the very thing behind the attacks and the subterfuge. But how to stop it? A flood of junk data filled Gerry's mind, sending bolts of pain through his brain. He couldn't stop the relentless torrent of images, audio, video.

"That's it. You've seen enough," Seca said. Then Gerry heard the clink of metal tools.

- *Shut it out, Mags. Cut the traffic!*

- *Activating firewalls. Disconnecting. Wait, there's a problem.*

- *What kind of problem?*

Gerry squeezed his eyes shut as the pain increased.

- *It knows… it knows what we are.*

- *I don't care. Disconnect.*

- *I can't. Seca has bridged the connection. I can't stop it.*

With great effort, Gerry envisioned the network and flow of traffic, focused on the connection between him and the AI, and coded a routing program, sending the data back out to the Meshwork. The demon AI responded instantly, re-routing around Gerry's roadblock, and so it went for minutes: Gerry spinning code, executing programs on-the-fly, the AI matching him, beating everything Gerry had. Then he realised. He and Mags might be as one, but they could work independently.

- Mags. Funnel the AI to Old Grey. She's on the Meshwork; I feel her.

While Mags shut down the computers and overloaded the various routers on the network so that the AI could only go straight to Old Grey, Gerry coded a simulation of himself. A virtual avatar representing himself within the network. He dropped the avatar into the flow of traffic and lured the demon AI. He knew Old Grey wasn't powerful enough to contain it, but she'd surely slow it down.

- Route is clear, executing virtual Gerry.

The demon AI knew what Gerry was trying to do, but wasn't given any other option. As quick as it tried to reboot the systems and routers on the Meshwork to give itself alternative paths, Gerry closed them down.

Sweat dripped from his forehead, covering his face. He tasted the salt on his lips and gripped his fists around the metal restraints as it took all his strength to concentrate and keep out the tendril-like programs of the AI.

A familiar presence appeared on the network. Old Grey responded to Gerry's request, and somehow he appealed to its curiosity, if such a thing existed within a computer being. It opened its ports and whatever it had in its systems, and the demon AI jumped at it entirely.

The Meshwork was silent then. Just the usual hum of low-level hackers looking for exploits and being casually rebuffed by router firewalls.

Outside of the network, and in real space, a clapping noise echoed around whatever room Gerry was in. He opened his eyes. Vision was returning to him, now that Mags was directing the NanoStems, but it wasn't perfect. Large amorphous blobs surrounded by halos of light hovered about him. By the echoing, he guessed he was in a room with metal floors and walls. The chill from beneath and around his wrists told him he was on a metallic bed of some sort.

The pain from his burned eye throbbed like a jackhammer into his skull.

The clapping continued until he felt the force of the expelled air right next to his ear.

"Who's a clever little thing? You're an intriguing man, Gerry. Some would say the Family's finest creation, though I wouldn't. You're flawed. Like the rest of us."

"Who is us exactly?"

A hand gripped his face, and a cloth wiped the sweat and tears from his good eye. After a few blinks, sharpness returned. Staring at him was something he could only describe as a robot's face. Sure, there was skin and eyes and all the rest of it, but they weren't human eyes, and behind the thin skin, bundles of wires and chips protruded from a brain. What human parts were there had been so spliced with technology that Gerry couldn't tell where the person finished and the tech started.

"You could consider me v1.0 Meta-human Beta. They called me Seca. Do you know why?"

"Enlighten me."

"My 'parents' once had a dog. They loved it very much. Until the day it got run over and broke all its legs and damaged its brain and central nervous system. He was the first to receive the groundbreaking technology that hybridised an animal brain and an intelligent computer program. The dog's name was Case. When he died, they wanted a new experiment, and I was born shortly after—imperfectly. It's an anagram. Just like I'm an anagram of a human and AI. Just like you are, Mr v2.0. Actually, that's not accurate. You must be version 50 by now. You see, I was a massive failure. Psychotic, they said. Unstable. So they dumped me, but I built myself back up, improved my software. I was better than anything they could ever build, including you."

"So why, then, are you stuck out here, hiding underground like a louse?"

The muscles in Seca's mouth twitched, exposing sharpened canine teeth and rotten molars.

"You think City Earth is a paradise? It's a prison. Nothing more than an experiment. You're all rats, running around to serve them. When they completed the Cataclysm, when they rid the world of governments and regulations, they built the Dome and the people in their own vision. They think they're gods!"

"And you think bringing the world to its knees under another war is going to change anything? Are you so desperate for mummy and daddy's approval you would kill thousands of innocent people?"

"Hah!" Seca spat with incredulity and stepped back, allowing more light in the room. "Innocent! Nothing on this earth is innocent. We're all just random collections of particles and energy. That was the secret to all of this. Understanding that information is just energy. Merging technology with the human consciousness was a trivial action once the mechanics were understood. Now, even street vendors are making their own. But the governments wouldn't allow it. Transhumanism was outlawed, but they didn't bank on the Family, and their resources, and their convictions. That's at least one thing I got from them: conviction."

"You're mad. Forgotten what it is to be human. Don't you have any shred of empathy left in you?"

"It died when they made me this."

Gerry squirmed and raised his head. He was alone in the room with Seca. The walls and floor were metal. A few metres to his left-hand side was a door. Seca's body, although covered by a baggy suit, was that of a withered, hunched twig. His face—entirely artificial—showed no age, but his hands were twisted with arthritis and muscular degeneration. Why hadn't he replaced those as well? Maybe he was clinging to his humanity after all. But the glaring, mechanised apertures of his eyes hid any compassion that might still be inside.

Gerry looked at his restraints, then the door.

Seca noticed and smiled with the sharp whirr of servos. As advanced as he was in terms of technology, he hadn't quite managed to replicate a sincere smile. Instead it looked like a grimace, as if smiling was painful.

"You're not going anywhere, Gerry. You'll die here. After I've opened you up and had a look at you more closely. You and your friends have played with things beyond your capability. But now you're here, I'm sure I can make use of you and that clever little AIA of yours."

"What have you done with Petal? The girl I was with."

"She's dead. As is that pathetic old man that sold you out for a software upgrade."

Gabe's betrayal hurt like a dagger to the chest, but paled into insignificance at the thought of Petal dead. Gerry slumped against the metal bed and shook with rage.

The anger built within Gerry like a high-pressured gas canister, squeezing everything else out, so all that remained was fury. He instructed Mags to overload the nearest node within Seca's network. If he was as hooked in as he appeared, he'd need Seca's network. Gerry could sense the flow of traffic from him, but couldn't penetrate the encryption, no matter how hard he analysed it for weakness. This was one battle he'd have to do the hard way.

- There's a nexus beyond the firewall, scanning for weakness, Mags said.

Gerry thrashed in his restraints, but they held firm. Then, as Seca removed a tray of medical tools from the side of the table, he noticed the restraints had no obvious mechanical fastening. They were electronic.

Seca hovered over the tray of sharp, steel implements. They weren't even clean. Dark brown stains and spots of rust covered their surfaces. He'd clearly done this kind of work before. A swell of panic added to Gerry's rage, and focusing his mind on Mags, he let himself drop into the flow of code. He lost all feeling of his physical body and felt as if he and Mags were a single entity again. He spotted the node hosting the firewall and crashed it, overloading its security and breaching it through an open port.

When he scanned it, he noticed it was the same port that Seca's encrypted data was using. Once beyond the firewall, he closed the port behind him, shutting Seca out of his own network.

Up ahead, four large AI-driven servers sorted data, processed billions of instructions and, on sensing him, sent out packets of malicious code. It stuck to him like a virus, the code mutating too fast for him to keep up with. Together, he and Mags coded a temporary shield. Held off the virus. Gerry then had an idea, but didn't know if it would kill him, Mags, or both in the process. Only one way to kill systems like these—an EMP. He had to fry the CPUs physically, but his consciousness was in the network. What would happen to him? Would it kill him, leaving his physical body just an inanimate piece of meat?

He was aware of something happening to his body. Skin being cut. Rough metal digging into bone. And laughing, Seca's sick, self-satisfied laugh as he cut into Gerry's skull.

Knowing Petal was dead and the demon AI would soon be in Jasper's possession, he didn't have much to lose. Seca would carve him up like a dead animal in a lab anyway, so he decided.

- *Mags, bring up a schematic of the power grid.*

- *Processing.*

A couple of seconds later, the image of the power layout was in Gerry's mind. He sent himself through a series of switches and gateways until he was at the node controlling the power supply. Seca had been lazy. The encryption algorithm on the power supply was an old one. Gerry hacked it within seconds. He quickly coded a new set of instructions for the power supply, increasing both amperage and voltage to deadly levels, deadly for tech at least. The code spun out of his mind as natural as breathing; he passed the software to the power supply's CPU and waited before executing the program.

The scraping against his skull increased, and he felt a saw raking back and forth as Seca determined to reach his brain.

Gerry could tell Seca was trying to figure out what he was doing as Seca breached his temporary barrier in the firewall, but unlike Gerry, it didn't seem as if he was as adept at multitasking. Still, Seca's code gained on him, battering against his shields.

So close now, in both cyberspace and real space, Seca was hacking into him, taking him apart. The viruses mutated again and grew in strength, but before they could take him down, Gerry executed the program and waited as a massive dump of electricity flooded the physical circuits that ran the servers.

An explosion blasted out. Waves of power vibrated through the walls of his room and into the board on which he was held.

Then silence.

Something hot trickled down his face and onto his lips: blood. Something slipped from his head and clattered onto the floor, followed by a heavy thud. Down to his right, the slumped body of Seca twitched in the dark gloom. Gerry pushed himself up on the table and managed to remove his wrists from the restraints that now lay open. He turned to his left; the door hung ajar. It seemed the EMP took out most of their security systems.

Swinging his legs off the metal bed made him vomit onto the floor. It was mostly bile and spit. Within the pool he saw a number of the writhing, black blobs: NanoStems. When he stood up, he realised what a job they'd done, as there was no pain in his ankle, and he stumbled around the bed to Seca's body. He was still, but his chest continued to rise and fall.

It took a while for him to accurately judge distances now that his right eye was ruined. He tentatively touched it and winced as a stab of pain crashed into his head. The agony fuelled his vengeance. He leant down, picked up the serrated blade that had just seconds ago scraped against his skull, and sliced it across Seca's throat until blood welled up in the wound.

From an internal speaker, Seca spoke. "Carve me up all you like! My consciousness will live on. I'll be one with the network."

"Screw you!"

The rage bubbled over. He stabbed at Seca again, this time in the chest, then the heart, the lungs, the stomach, the kidneys. He kept stabbing until he screamed and the lactic acid in his arm muscles prevented him from slicing at the dead meat anymore.

He slumped backwards, tears rushing down his face.

The blade shook in his hand, now entirely covered in dark red blood. The room looked like a slaughterhouse. The stink made him retch over and over as he crawled away on hands and knees.

When he reached the door, he pulled himself up on the handle and shuffled out into the corridor. He felt entirely alone—again. Mags wasn't responding, and his brain felt like mush. Coherent thoughts were slow coming, and he even had trouble thinking of his name. How much had he lost in the EMP? It was too difficult to understand right now. All he could think of was escape. Had to find a way out, find a way of stopping... what was his name?

It wouldn't come, but he knew there was a man at home waiting for something, to deliver something, and it was up to him to stop it.

Chapter 18

For what seemed like hours or days, Gerry—for his brain managed to dredge his name up from the murky depths—shuffled through the dark corridors of Seca's sanctuary. He didn't recognise any of it. Even the way he'd come in was lost to his foggy memory.

He knew he must be getting close, however. A rumble from above shook the metal walls, and he shuffled towards it as best he could, climbing access ladders to higher levels and walking down yet more corridors. Some were filled with the inanimate bodies of Seca's guards. It seemed none were wholly human. It occurred to him that there were probably more cyborgs, robots and transcendents than human beings in the world now. Maybe even he didn't count? And yet he was still walking.

I must be human, then, he thought. I'm a human. I'm a human. He rumbled the thought around his head until it became a mantra, the rhythm of the syllables matching his lurching strides.

A metallic grating noise, followed by a loud rush of air blasted down from above him. It was dusk out, but a strong white light flickered across the hole in the roof, blinding him in its brilliance. A shadow appeared in the glare and dropped down a rope.

Gerry dived out of the way as a humanoid—for he couldn't be sure what it was; nothing was sure anymore—landed with a thud. It was a female shape, with tall pink hair... so familiar. A word tried to form on his lips as he pressed them together.

She spun, shining a torch in his eyes, and he scuttled back into the shadows.

"Gez? That you?"

He knew that voice, and still the name wouldn't come. His voice wouldn't come.

She shined the torch to one side and crouched down as she approached. She wore goggles over her eyes and plasters across her right cheek. A crimson slash arced through the beige material.

"Gez. It's me, Petal. Are you hurt?"

She bent down closer, and Gerry breathed in her scent. She smelled of soap and medical alcohol. A flashback memory flickered in his mind of a man leaning over him with a bottle of alcohol. No. It was something else. A cure of some kind for his wounds. Gerry reached up to touch his nose and felt rough skin as if a scab had recently healed.

The girl held out her hand, and he took it, encapsulating it entirely. She was small, petite, but she had strength to her. He did know her. Flashes of her face came to him in blinking fragments, but it was all too indistinct.

"Come on, we've got to get you back to City Earth. Old Grey couldn't hold it, and Jasper's still roaming free. I managed to get the Jaguar back from Len. I don't know what you did back there, but the whole city went down. You must have taken out the entire power grid. Len thought it was his payload and came into the city… I managed to get out, but I couldn't find you. Gez, say something. Speak to me."

"P… P… Petal?"

"Yeah, Gez. Petal, remember? We came here to stop Seca… stop the AI… what did you do?"

He looked at her blankly. The name Seca didn't mean anything to him, and what AI? All he remembered was the pain in his head, and the body. The body he butchered. He closed his eyes, trying to erase that particular, gory image. Of all the things he could have remembered, why did it have to be that?

The girl sighed and pulled him to the rope. She looped it twice around his waist and made him grip it as best he could. She flashed the torch up through the hole. The rumbling increased, pulling him up and out of his underground prison. He dropped his head back as he breached the surface. The cool air stung his wounds, but he breathed it deeply, taking the rich oxygen into his lungs.

The winch whirred as it lifted him up through a gap beneath the aircraft. A chrome-masked man reached out a hand and pulled him into a seated area.

"You did great. Whatever it is was. You knocked out Seca's operation completely. My payload didn't do anything that I expected. His security was too hot, but you, however, you managed it! The man hugged Gerry before sitting back on the bench seat.

"Who are you?" Gerry asked.

"Your ticket home, friend."

They dropped the winch and brought Petal up. She sat next to the grinning man and stared at Gerry with the same look of awe. He couldn't understand their reactions. Had no idea what they were talking about or what he had supposedly done. But instinctively he knew it was important, and there was something else he needed to do. He just hoped by the time he got where he was going that he could remember what it was.

As they gained altitude and picked up speed, Gerry watched the sun dip below the horizon. Thick, bulbous clouds carrying the promise of water covered the moon. He wished for rain. Wished for everything to be washed away and started anew.

Petal took a medical pack from the bulkhead behind her seat. She kneeled beside Gerry and, taking a cleansing wipe, began to clean his cuts. Looking at her wound—a fierce gash below her eye—he knew within himself that he'd let her down, failed to protect her. Someone had tasked him with her care, and now she was the one caring for him.

A roiling anger crawled around his guts like a snake awakening from a deep sleep. Angry because he'd failed her, but also for those who'd hurt her. Flashes of faces came to him, and each time he tried to focus, they blinked away, hiding on the edge of consciousness. But a name came to him: Jasper.

"Who's Jasper?" he asked.

"The guy we're gonna kill," Petal replied, fixing a series of plasters to his wounds. "He is the one who has the demon AI you tried to stop. Or at least will have it soon."

'Tried.' The word was like a knife slicing into his heart. She didn't say it with any malice, but it was yet another reminder that whatever had gone down, he had failed her.

Failed to stop this AI.

"I won't fail again," Gerry whispered. He pictured an image of Jasper. He was standing intimately with a woman, someone who used to be close to Gerry. My wife! And then he relived the moment again. The video played over in his mind of his wife betraying him.

The snake slithered further throughout his body, and he focused on what he was going to do. He pictured the bloody scene back in that metal room. The room of the body and the blood, and he pictured Jasper's face on that mutilated lump of meat. All Gerry wanted then was vengeance.

Chapter 19

Petal filled Gerry in on what had happened. Their missions, Gabe's betrayal, and what Jasper was planning to do. His memory didn't feel like his own anymore. His AIA wasn't responding—presumably killed by the EMP attack. Still, he felt ready to do what was necessary. He had children, and fragments of their lives and their time together lurked in the shadows of his mind, growing ever stronger, so that he now felt the loss of separation almost as strongly as his desire for revenge.

Channelling that loss fuelled his motivation. His focus. He'd lost so much lately, and he would rather die trying to restore order and save his city, as false and unreal as it was, than stand back and watch a million innocent people suffer at the hands of a fundamentalist and an AI programmed for evil.

That the Family were equally evil in their actions wasn't the point anymore. He couldn't undo the massive loss of life during the Cataclysm, and he couldn't undo what the Family had done to the people living inside the Dome. But he could at least try and give them time. Time to live their lives as they'd always done: with ignorance and security. They were nothing more than lab rats for the amusement of a group of megalomaniac and wannabe gods, but they were still his people, and he was determined to give them as much chance of a secure life as possible.

Jasper and the AI had to be stopped.

A mask-wearing pilot spoke over their comm system. "Approaching the Dome. Security's out in force. Eight squadrons of assault drones coming our way."

"Hold on, Gez. This could get bumpy." Petal pulled the safety straps on his flight jacket tight, pulling him securely into his seat. Gerry reached out and did the same, ensuring Petal was as secure as he was.

"Isn't this a suicide mission? Shouldn't we have called ahead? Explained to the Family what's happening?" Gerry said. Outside the window, he saw a group of drones shaped like birds dart in formation to flank their craft.

"We tried that. Jasper's got the place on lockdown. No traffic to and from the Family's space station. It'll take hours for them to get reinforcements to the ground, and we don't have the luxury. But don't worry. I managed to get a message to the prez. Let's just hope he believed me."

The side of her mouth kinked up, creating a sly, knowing grin.

It quickly changed as their craft jolted violently.

"Ion blasts! We can't take many of these. I thought you uploaded the new codes?" Len said, staring at Petal.

Another explosion and they began to spin. Gerry's guts twisted, and he gripped the handholds above his head. The smell of superheated ions brought back a memory of him being chased down by a drone... of being stuck, covered in steaming hot mud after narrowly avoiding an explosion

"Try the codes again," Len shouted.

Petal was already one step ahead, frantically entering data on her HackSlate. "It's no good. Jasper's blocked my access to the drones. He must have got to Kuznetski. I don't have time to hack my way in…"

Gerry reached across and took the HackSlate from her. The streams of code on the display resonated with him. He'd seen instructions like this before. It was written in Helix++, and he knew the AI, with its loops-within-loops of ever-changing programs. His hands began to move of their own accord. Everything but the code faded to black, and he felt himself disconnect from reality. All that existed was his mind and the code.

First he took control of the Jaguar and programmed an evasion route, sending their craft higher and higher. The drones followed, keeping up with their speed. The Dome shrunk beneath them as they climbed further.

In the real world, someone gripped his arm, shouted something, but he paid no attention. He was one with the code now, and he manipulated a set of commands to send the craft back down towards the Dome in a wide arcing corkscrew pattern.

As they passed the drones, they fired, but their speed was too great, and they missed. The G-force pushed Gerry back into his seat, and he could feel the reverberations of explosions behind him as the drones either crashed into each other or were caught in the crossfire.

The Dome was no more than half a kilometre away. He could hear panic in the voices as they screamed at him, but he ignored their protests and sent the craft into a straight dive.

Gerry accessed the weapons subroutine and fired their

two on-board missiles after deactivating their payloads. He didn't want the explosion, just the penetration. They launched towards their target, and Gerry tracked their trajectory so that they flanked the craft ten metres either side of its hull. They pierced through the Plexiglas outer shell of the Dome, and the Jaguar followed, easily breaking through the weakened material.

The drones, however, didn't have the manoeuvrability and stuck in their spiral descent, crashed against the exterior, smashing to pieces.

Gerry brought the craft into a slow dip before levelling out. He flew it across the fields of GreenWay Park and through a series of downtown districts. Accessing the city's metro maps, he followed the magno-tracks towards the main Council district where President Kuznetski had his office. They'd arrive in less than a minute, which gave him time to search the network and assess the damage.

Petal was right. Jasper had blocked traffic from coming in or leaving the Dome. It was like the demon AI had entangled the entire place in thick impenetrable tentacles. He saw no way through. The sheer depth and complexity of the viral barrier attacked anything that got near it. He backed off and ran a series of identity searches. One of the benefits of the city and everyone's inbuilt AIAs was that anyone could be found and traced.

First he checked his kids: both were alive and at their last address. He presumed they were safe—for now at least. He left a trace program running on them to alert him of their movements. Next he searched for his wife. Predictably, she wasn't on the network, and neither was Jasper. Obviously he was cloaking them both within the confines of the AI.

Last, he checked the president and found him. Only his warning beacon was sending out alert messages. Code 1: the highest possible emergency. But it was no use; they just bounced back off the AI. At least he had a lock on his position.

Gerry set the coordinates and pulled himself out of the code. It took him a few seconds to readjust. Petal and Len both stared at him, their faces glossy with panic sweat.

"You crazy, man!" Petal said with a grin so wide Gerry could see all her teeth, before leaning forward and kissing him on the cheek.

Len just shook his head. "I don't know how you do what you do."

Gerry looked at him, thought for a while, and said with a serious tone, "Neither do I."

They entered the presidential building. Len's holograms led the procession, their laser barrier giving them easy access. The security team didn't know what to make of them. They'd obviously not seen anything like it. And the fact that Gerry, the most wanted man in City Earth, was alive and in their midst shocked them into silence.

The route was quick and easy. The government nerve centre hadn't really needed much better security. This was the Dome, after all—where people do as they're told and aren't given any reason to complain or protest.

Gerry approached the chamber doors to Kuznetski's personal room. He didn't stop to knock. Just kicked open the doors and approached the great, polished oak desk that the president was sitting over, head in his hands. His bald head shined with sweat under the lights. Patches of grey and brown on his sides were turning greyer than Gerry had remembered when he last saw him giving a public address a couple of weeks ago.

"They've gone," Kuznetski said, looking up at Gerry. Heavy bags hung beneath his brown eyes, and the wrinkles around his eyes and mouth had deepened to rough crags.

"Who's gone?" Gerry asked.

"Those who are taking the City from me."

"We've come to help."

"Who are you people?" He sat back from his desk then, taking in the scene in detail for the first time.

The elder man looked closely at Gerry for a few long seconds. A shine of recognition lit up his dark brown eyes. "How did you... you should be..."

"Dead. I know. Look, we haven't got time for this. Just tell me what happened."

Miralam Kuznetski slumped in his chair and rubbed his forehead. Gerry could almost hear the cogitations going through his brain. He looked up at Gerry then, regarded him and his entourage closely, and then leant forward on the desk.

"Okay. They came, took the security codes and left. I couldn't stop them. It happened too quickly. My security... we're not set up... how was I—"

"You couldn't have done anything. Don't blame yourself. Just tell me what you know about them and where they're heading. We'll take over from here."

He hesitated, scanning Gerry and his allies. Gerry knew they must have looked like a ragtag outfit. Gerry stepped forward, leaned over the desk and stared Kuznetski in the eyes.

"Listen," Gerry said, keeping his voice calm, friendly. "I need you to trust us. I could spend some time showing you evidence of what's going on, giving you the rundown of everything that I, and my allies here, have gone through in order to get here, but frankly I'm tired, stressed, and we're running out of time. I need you to tell me where they went, and right now. Okay?"

It was clear to Gerry the man was out of his depth. Sweat dripped from his forehead, and his jaw hung open. A vein pulsed in his temple.

"Come on, man," Petal said. "We're trying to help you here. Just tell us."

Miralam wiped the sweat from his face, sat back and took in a deep breath. "Okay," he said. "They went to Cemprom."

Gerry thought back through his murky memories to his time there. So many faces flew through his thoughts, and one stuck out. His boss. Mike Welling. His brain filled in the rest, rebuilding old connections, bridging memories and building a mosaic of dread. His right hand twitched as he remembered firing the gun that put Mike out of his misery.

"The AIAs! Have they got into them yet?" Gerry asked.

Kuznetski squinted at Gerry. "What do you mean?"

"Jasper, the guy who is leading all this, wants to access the main city network to get to everyone's AIA. Once he's inside, he could wipe out every single person in this city…"

Kuznetski didn't say anything. Just sat back in his chair and ran a shaking hand across his bald head. "They've abandoned me here, haven't they?"

"They? Who are you talking about?" Gerry asked. "Wait, you're one of the Family too?"

He nodded. "I'd hoped they would have received my alert signal. They should have come by now. But I'm stuck here."

Petal stepped up beside Gerry. "Wait a god-damned minute," she said, pointing her finger at Kuznetski. "If you're one of the Family, then you must know Jasper."

"No, no, I don't. I've never been up to the station. He only came down a few months ago. I didn't even know about it until recently. I don't know him."

Gerry held up his hand. It was clear he was telling the truth. The guy was panicked almost out of his skin. His hands shook like he had frostbite, and he physically pushed himself back away from Petal as she leaned towards him.

"I don't care about you right now." Gerry couldn't hide his disdain for him and the Family. He fought to control the rising fury within himself. It seemed that Kuznetski's connection to the Family wasn't just through his father's relationship with them during the war. It was clear that Kuznetski Senior was closer to the Family than most had known. "I need to know why Jasper's gone to Cemprom. Is that where the main node is?"

"Yes, the central uplink. It's in the underground secure room. No one but the Family and I knew about it. Not even you guys who worked on the algorithms and the security systems. It was supposed to be a completely ring-fenced safety measure. In case it got hacked, it was supposed to keep—"

"The Family safe? Yeah, that much is evident. Give me the codes. Now."

Kuznetski took a DigiCard from his jacket pocket and handed it over to Gerry, who passed it on to Petal.

"Can you check that, Petal?" Gerry said.

She took the card, nodded, and inserted it into her HackSlate. While she was doing that, Gerry turned back to Kuznetski.

"How long ago did they leave?"

"About ten minutes. I can get you there quicker, though. We have a direct access tunnel here under the building. Not on any schematics so they didn't know about it, didn't even ask. Jasper seemed frantic, unfocused."

"Yeah, coz Gez here screwed his boss right up, and he's running scared, that's why," Petal said.

Gerry couldn't help but crack the barest of smiles at her petulance and utter disregard for authority. He was reminded all over again why he liked her so much.

"The codes are good, Gez," Petal said.

"Good. Len, can you leave some of your guys here to make sure Mr President doesn't do anything stupid?"

"Hey, I'm on your—"

"You're most definitely not on my side," Gerry said as he leaned across the desk, violating his personal space. "You could have killed my kids today with your pathetic actions. Make no mistake. Whatever happens, I will be back to deal with you personally."

Kuznetski slunk back in his chair, quivering as he swallowed.

"Consider it done," Len said as he gestured to his hologram guards. Four of them stationed themselves in each corner of the room. They raised their arms to shoulder height, and a line of lasers connected from one hand to the other, securing the room.

"Show us the tunnel," Gerry demanded.

The elder man nearly tripped as he rose from his chair and hurried across the polished wood floor to a section of wall. He pressed his hand against the surface and spoke aloud a series of numbers. A red LED light shone from the wall and scanned his face. There was a click from a mechanism, and the wall dropped into the ground. Ahead of them, a precisely cut square tunnel stretched off into the distance. On the floor was a single track.

He tapped at a control panel attached to the wall inside the tunnel. From within the darkness an amber light shone. It grew brighter as Gerry heard the telltale hum of a magno-train.

The white plastic carriage came to a silent stop at the head of the access way. "This'll take you across the City to Cemprom HQ in less than two minutes. When you get there, you'll need this." Kuznetski handed Gerry a round disc the size of an antique dollar.

"You'll find a single slot at the end of the tunnel. Put this in, and you'll get access to the elevator that will take you directly to the server room. You should get there before Jasper and his people. To get there through the Cemprom building is tricky and time-consuming. There's just a single ladder that goes down for half a kilometre."

"Hopefully you can protect it from this AI. It can't be taken offline, so you'll need to find another way."

"You better not be lying about any of this. Len's security detail is more than capable of slicing you into pieces no bigger than this disc." By the look on his face, Gerry knew he was being sincere. Sweat continued to drip from his face, and unsightly wet patches circled beneath his arms.

"I promise you, Mr Cardle, I want you to succeed as much as you do."

"Tell me. I'm a dead man according to the system, aren't I?"

"The lottery algorithm considered you a winner. It's in the records."

"Good. I want it to stay that way."

Before the president had a chance to say anything else, Gerry pushed him aside, opened the door to the magno-train, and waited for Len and Petal to take their seats.

"Right. Let's go, then. We've got a demon to exorcise."

The circular nature of being on another train, heading towards another uncertain future wasn't lost on Gerry. The memory and the reality merged into one, and as the train pulled away, he did the same as before: watched the light of his past diminish to a dot and finally disappear into blackness. He was dead to the city. Nothing more than a ghost.

There was only forward now.

Len looked at Gerry, then Petal, and saw their stern expressions.

"What have I got myself into?"

Both Petal and Gerry together said, "The Salvation business, man."

Gerry let Petal finish off with: "The pay's crap, but the satisfaction is good for the soul."

Despite Petal's smile, the fact Gabe wasn't here with them left a hollow feeling inside Gerry's chest. How could he sell them out? He didn't want to believe it, but couldn't think of a logical alternative.

Chapter 20

The president was right. The train took them to Cemprom, and the elevator lowered them to the server room in just a few minutes. The place was quiet, as anything a half a kilometre beneath the earth was. It reminded him of a tomb. He pushed the thought aside and assessed the situation.

The room was lit evenly by strip lighting and reminded Gerry of one of Enna's medical facilities as his memories continued to return to him.

The server itself was surprisingly small and located centrally on a steel plinth.

Petal scanned the room with her HackSlate, looking for rogue traffic signatures trying to access the server: there was nothing. Nothing but the single stream of data flowing into the city's network from this server. It was all one way. The server was responsible for the AIA management, and given its size, Gerry knew there must be something special about it, considering the size of the computing power to run a network and track everything across a million citizens.

She scanned the DigiCard and sent the codes across the VPN to Gerry.

"Let's see what she's got inside," Gerry said as he took a cable from his duster jacket and plugged himself into the machine. When he clicked the jack-plug into his neck port, there was none of the usual buzz of information. It was smooth as butter.

He entered the codes, and to his relief, the credentials were good. He was logged in and looking at a terminal window.

"How's it looking, Gez?" Petal asked.

"Not sure yet. I'm still finding my feet. Len, can you watch the entrance in case we get interrupted?"

"Sure thing." Len opened his coat and took two pistols from his holsters. He crouched below the entranceway and aimed his guns up into the darkness.

The server had a very basic interface. The first thing Gerry wanted to do was make sure it hadn't been compromised. He ran a number of diagnostic checks and was presented with a set of log files. Scanning these, he was relieved to see that it wasn't on the same system as Jasper's evil AI as he couldn't feel that impenetrable mutating code trying to violate him, nor see any peculiar access requests. But still he had to make sure that the city's citizens were okay.

He started to enter a set of commands that he'd used regularly in his job at Cemprom when designing the algorithm. It was a group of applications that scanned, recorded, and accounted for each individual. He launched them, entered more of the requested access codes, and was presented with a report. Gerry relaxed into the analysis of the data, finding his Zen moment and spinning out queries with his mind as quick as thoughts. The server complied and delivered its results:

No AIAs were damaged thus far.

Everything was normal.

No compromises.

Jasper's AI had tried to get in from the wider city network, but the server was completely safe from external traffic. The only way in was direct. Gerry could try to programme some kind of defence in case Jasper managed to get access to it, but the complexity of the AI was too large for him to keep out. The only way to ensure the citizens' complete safety was to destroy the server. Society would lose its connection to the network and the benefits of their personal AIAs, but at least they'd be alive, and free.

Searching the power supply and the city's grid, he had to rule out an EMP. The server was behind several heavy-duty EMP protection circuits. He couldn't just unplug the machine either, as it was fixed, as one, to the steel column and had a number of back-up energy sources, including the room itself. The walls acted as wireless energy transfer units. He even suspected that this wasn't even the central processing unit. The computing power was distributed. There could be hundreds of these somewhere, all providing redundancy in a cloud formation.

Taking it offline was not an option.

Of course, they could just kill Jasper and his pals, but then that wouldn't solve the problem of getting rid of the AI from the wider network. No, he'd have to lure them into a trap.

It had to stop here.

As he was formulating a workable plan, a shattering noise woke him from his trance.

Gunfire erupted from further up in the tunnel to reverberate around the small room.

Len managed to get two shots off before a volley of lead obliterated his face, sending him crashing to the floor in pieces.

Gerry grabbed Petal and pushed her behind the column. He picked up one of Len's pistols, crouched to the side of the column, and waited for the first body to come down the ladder.

"You don't really have anywhere to go, Gerry. Your time is up. I'll give it you. You exceeded all expectations. Who would have thought little Gerry would have been capable of so much? Our parents would be so proud, but such a shame the only thing they'll get now is bits of your body in a casket. Unless you cooperate with me, of course. It's not too late—brother."

"Jasper? What are you on about?" Could he really be his brother, and his parents—still alive?

A black-clothed man dropped from the tunnel on a zip line and rolled to avoid Gerry's first shot. He knelt up, pointed a gun at Gerry, and yelled, "Put it down, Gerry, and you might survive the day."

Gerry didn't hesitate and shot the man in the face, spraying parts of his skull up the wall. The heat of the shot boiled the blood so that a red mist fell upon the slumped body.

"I've got many more of them, brother. We could do this all day until you're out of ammo, which by my reckoning will be in two more shots. Low capacity on those pistols, you see."

"I was an only child! My parents never alluded to

anything otherwise. Not to mention they're dead. Now shut up and come down here and face me. Let's end this."

Gerry logged out of the system and wiped his access file to remove the codes.

Jasper laughed as another body slipped down the ladder. This time Gerry wasn't quick enough, and the woman ducked his shot, rushed him, and drove him to the floor.

Gerry fired the pistol, but it struck the ceiling.

A fist crashed into his face, breaking his nose and dislodging the cable and connection to the server.

The pain blinded him for a second as old wounds split open. He slumped back, twisting his head to avoid swallowing blood. Another heavy punch pounded into his skull. Gerry's head bounced off the metal floor. His world spun. His body tensed with a racking pain.

The woman's steel-covered fist rose up ready to bring down another blow, but her head jerked back violently, and blood spilled from her neck.

Petal pulled her spike out, thrust it again into the woman's chest, and kicked her to one side.

"Gez, you okay?" Petal asked. She knelt over him, her hands on his face. "Gez!"

Gerry gurgled, "I'm... okay..." as he sat up.

There was a noise like the clatter of boots on metal and the whirring of zip lines. Gerry looked up.

Standing in front of him was Jasper, backed up by five men and women in black clothing and holding heavy weaponry. The tiny pistol, now next to him, seemed entirely ineffective in comparison, but it didn't stop Petal from reaching over to grab it and levelling it at Jasper's face.

"Pull the trigger, little girl," he said with a sly grin.

She did. Nothing happened. Out of ammo.

"I did warn you. You should have paid attention." Jasper gestured to a woman next to him, and she shot Petal in the leg, sending her spinning to the ground.

"Strap and bag her. She's coming with us."

"Leave her alone!" Gerry made to stand, but a heavy boot from one of Jasper's goons pushed down on his throat, pinning him uselessly to the floor like a bug.

Two more of Jasper's squad strode around the server.

Petal lashed out at one of them, catching him in the face with her spike, but another goon had already removed a netted bag and quickly subdued her. They tied her up and pulled her away from Gerry.

Jasper gestured to the man with a boot pressed at Gerry's throat. The boot lifted, allowing Gerry to take a choking breath. Gerry rose to his feet with an overwhelming desire to kill every last person in the room, but he was impotent to do anything. Unarmed and injured, backed into a corner, he had nothing left to offer. Unless what Jasper said was true. If he were his brother, then he'd be like Gerry. He'd be able to…

Backing away with his arms up, Gerry scrutinised Jasper. He had to be honest with himself. They certainly shared a resemblance. He recognised those eyes and the bone structure. There was one way to find out.

"Okay, let's all just stop and think about this," Gerry said, trying to buy time, allowing his mind and body to recover from the violence so that he could think straight. Then he thought about his and Petal's VPN connection. His dermal implant was still active. In the back of his mind it blinked away, waiting for instruction.

"Take her up," Jasper said.

Two of his people attached the zip line to Petal and sent her up into the tunnel. They followed behind, leaving Jasper and just two of his guards. That made the odds a little more even. Jasper moved to the server, took a slate from his pocket, and plugged in the trailing cable from the server. He turned to one of his people. "The codes?"

He fished around his flak jacket, checking his numerous pockets like a best man at a wedding trying to find the rings. He eventually pulled out a DigiCard and handed it to Jasper, who gestured expertly across the slate's surface.

"I see you've had a bit of an upgrade," Jasper said, referring to Gerry's neck port.

"I code better with a direct connection."

Jasper laughed, shaking his head. "If only you knew. I fear it's too late, though. You have the expression of a radical. You're too far gone."

"For what?"

Jasper ignored him. "You did quite the job on Seca. I saw it on the video feed. A little bit stabby, aren't you? I wonder where you get that from?"

"If you're trying to say we're alike, then you're far madder than I thought."

"Aren't we both killers? Haven't we both done extreme things for those we love?"

"You don't love anything. That's why you're willing to slaughter an entire city."

"They're an abomination. I'm doing this for humanity."

"Even if that means killing my kids? They're your family too, after all." He hoped that would have some effect, but

Jasper just smiled and shook his head.

"They're not your kids, Gerry. Just surrogates to keep you in your place. Just like your wife isn't your wife, but a defected agent. She works for me now. Good in bed too, huh?"

As much as it hurt, Gerry wanted to keep him talking, buy more time. While Jasper carried on with his taunts, Gerry accessed his VPN. No response from Petal, which was to be expected. At least she was still alive. He scanned the room and found the IP addresses of Jasper and his guards. As he'd hoped, they too were sharing a VPN for communications. He directed his implant's transmitter to one of Jasper's men's comm unit and was blocked by the firewall.

"If things were different, you could have helped me take down the Family, make them pay for what they've done. We wouldn't have had to be enemies over this. Even Seca was just a pawn to be extinguished. You and I could have given humanity a fresh start. One without interference…"

Gerry nodded, kept eye contact and watched Jasper grow ever more animated as he tried to access the server. It was taking longer than it should. He hoped Kuznetski had given him the wrong codes.

"If you are my brother, why did it take so long for you to tell me? You were at Cemprom for a while, why not say something then?"

Gerry continued to probe the firewall as he kept Jasper talking. He noticed a particular port in the firewall open up to receive a message from another member of the team. Gerry noted the signature and encryption code of the data stream, replicated it, and programmed a Helix self-replicating exploit.

It slipped through, and he felt the connection. One more bridge to get to Jasper...

Jasper looked down at his slate quizzically and entered more data as his face began to redden. He glared at Gerry.

"What have you done?"

Gerry didn't know if he meant the server or his trying to access his VPN connection. "You're the genius here. You tell me."

Jasper flared his nostrils and turned to the woman on his left carrying a pistol. "Shoot him in the leg."

Almost before he finished the command, the woman pulled the trigger while wearing a smile on her face. Gerry collapsed to the floor as a slug smashed his knee to pulp. He gripped the mess with his hands, stifled the scream, and shut his eyes as he wished for the pain to pass. But it continued to build. Searing heat travelled up his leg, burning every nerve ending as it went.

"Now, give me the codes, or I'll take the other leg," Jasper said.

Gerry pointed to Petal's HackSlate on the floor. That Jasper hadn't noticed it before was a good sign. He was distracted.

Inside Gerry's head something tingled, and he smiled. Mags was back.

- *Mags, what happened?*

- *The EMP fried some of your neural paths. The latent NanoStems have repaired them, and I'm back online. The pain you experience was just what I needed to get going again. Shall we get to work?*

He felt complete again and, despite the pain, focused

his mind on the task at hand. Together, his mind and his AIA spun code as one, easily skipping across the bridge and into Jasper's comm unit.

- *Wait until he downloads the AI into the system, and then execute program #081,* Gerry said.

Program #081 was his lure, and he hoped he had just enough time to make it work.

- *Execution ready.*

Lying in the corner of the room, Gerry's heart skipped a beat, becoming irregular. He thought he was dying. It didn't seem like his heart would stand the stress, yet he pushed himself further, sending his mind into the stream of Helix code once again. Through Jasper's comm unit, he watched as his brother downloaded the colossal AI. Its black, writhing tentacles of multithreaded viral code swarmed the CPU, penetrating its defences as though they were nothing more than paper soldiers.

- *Launch the program, Mags.*

He hoped with what he thought were his final breaths that he'd got it right. He didn't have time to debug the code or test the program. It was literally all or nothing.

- *Successfully executed, awaiting report. I'm switching off your pain receptors and directing what's left of the NanoStems to your heart. Hold out for a while longer; we can't die just yet.*

- *I'm... trying...*

A black fog snuffed out his view of the network and the flow of data. He felt the icy touch of an AI's multithreaded virus enter his brain. This wasn't how it should have happened. The AI was probing his brain, leaving malicious code in its wake, destroying cells and neural pathways.

Gerry was sure he could hear an audio file of something laughing as it took him apart piece by piece.

Old memories came flooding back: images of past birthdays with his wife and kids. Walking the dog in the fields, and then he was younger, trying on badly designed jumpers, and there, opposite him, another child wearing the same jumper. It was true...

Two high-pitched screams broke through his consciousness. The two guards fell to the floor, blood pouring from their ears and noses. Jasper reeled away from the server, dropping his slate. Across the VPN connection, Jasper screamed and shouted 'no' over and over. The Helix code running to and from the VPN transformed and mutated as the AI's subroutines investigated this change.

- *Disconnect us from the VPN now, Mags.*

- *Disconnection successful.*

The set of preprogrammed instructions executed, and the AI leapt from his brain and into the nearest node: Jasper.

Gerry's heart stopped. At first he thought it was because he wasn't breathing, but when he took in a deep breath and rapidly filled and emptied his lungs in attempt to start his heart again, it remained quiet and still. The last dark, tentacular viruses of the AI were easy to uninstall from his brain.

- *What happened? Did it work?*

- *Yes, but we're dying.*

He closed his eyes, thought of his kids, and lay very still as Jasper's data flow stopped. Everything was quiet, and life slipped away as one by one Gerry's organs failed. At the very end, the last thing to stop working was his brain.

It was clean. He'd successfully managed to exorcise the demon AI—by using Jasper as the lure. To save his family, he had to sacrifice his own brother. He made peace with it and let the darkness take him. At least the city was safe.

Chapter 21

The afterlife wasn't something Gerry believed in. He was having trouble explaining why he could still feel and hear. Maybe he was still actually dying and, as the blood ran from his brain, phantom stimuli tricked him into thinking everything was okay.

His right hand dangled down, and his fingers brushed against something soft. Carpet perhaps. No. It moved. He twitched his fingers away, but the furry thing pushed against him, purring. He realised it was a cat. A real cat!

He opened his mouth, felt the dryness within his throat, but was still able to speak. "Hello? Is someone here? Where am I?"

The purring continued as the cat nudged against his hand before leaping up beside him. It curled against him, and its purr vibrated through his chest. It was soothing, and soon he felt his own breathing match the rhythm of the cat. He tried to open his eyes, but something held them shut. This couldn't be the afterlife, could it?

A door opened. Footsteps shuffled across the carpet. "Are you awake?"

It was a female voice, soft, but with a mature tone.

"Who are you? Where am I?"

She cupped his left hand in hers. They were soft and warm, and only then did he realise how cold he was. "I'm your mother, and you're home, my darling."

She peeled away the tape holding the bandages to his eyes, and light flooded in. In the brightness, he saw a woman standing beside him. She was tall, lithe, and glowing with vitality. Her eyes were bright blue, her skin, completely flawless. She turned away from him and opened the blinds on the window. Outside, distant stars studded the great black space. And then he noticed, in the corner of the window, a blue planet moving slowly across their path in an arc. Earth.

"My girls?" Gerry asked.

"Safe. You saved everyone, apart from your brother. But Gerry, my son, don't fret. They're not your girls anymore. Never were, but I know your love was real. That's why we believed in you. Unlike all our other children, you were the one with empathy. You were the most human. But I'm afraid you're badly damaged, and we have to rebuild you."

"Rebuild? What happened to me?"

"You died. But don't worry, we'll soon make you better than before, and then you'll be going back to Earth."

"Where exactly am I?"

"Our space station, of course. Like I said, Gerry love, you're home." She wiped his forehead with a cloth and smiled at him. "We need you to go back and do one more thing for us."

"I've died for you! Been tortured for you! What more can I give?"

"You met a girl calling herself Petal. We need her. She's ill, and we can't allow her to die."

"What do you know about her?"

"She's living evolution, Gerry. And dangerous."

"Dangerous how?"

"You've seen what she can do, holding code secure. Well, she can do that to DNA too. She can hold a human consciousness within her and mutate it. In the wrong hands… well, let's just say that you thought Seca was out of control, he would pale into insignificance if our enemies get hold of the girl and realise what she can do."

"And who are your enemies? In fact, it seems everyone is your enemy. I can't say I blame them, considering what you did during the Cataclysm."

"Ah, the Cataclysm. They all think it was us. Well, that's not entirely true. We ended it, Gerry, but it was the governments that started it. They were the ones to first drop the nukes. They sent hundreds of thousands of drones into civilised areas and killed millions of innocent people. If we hadn't stepped in when we did, there would be nothing at all left. That's why we built the Dome. To start again. To give humanity a fighting chance."

"And in the process, forsake all those outside it."

She lowered her head then. Her sadness clear and apparently genuine.

"We tried to help them. They're too far gone. If we let them in, the gene pool would fragment and wither. We can't allow that. We need to build a stronger, more resistant human. It's a harsh world out there, Gerry. You've not even scratched the surface, but we'll teach you. We'll show you everything, and then, my dear, we'll rebuild you and send you back so you can find your Petal."

The way she said it: 'your Petal,' as if they were more

than just casual acquaintances. And yet she was right. He knew it. He loved her, in some way. If what his mother was saying was true, he would kill for the chance to go back and find her. And Gabe. There was bad blood there that needed letting. One way or another.

"What do you plan on doing with her if I agree to do what you ask?"

"Keep her safe. The pair of you can live here, in perfect safety. Your every desire and want can be catered for here. Even more so than the Dome. You will be a free man here. Free to come and go as you please. You could have a wonderful life. Our research departments would be at your disposal. You could continue your work or go in any other direction you wish."

"What if I wanted to stay down there?"

"You won't, Gerry. When you experience what it's really like, when you go to the places that we suspect Petal has been taken to, you really won't want to stay there."

"And what about my girls? I still miss them." But even as he finished that sentence, to his surprise, he realised that wasn't entirely true. He barely knew them now. Or his wife. That world seemed so far away. As if it all took place in a dream, fading into his memories. Was that the doing of this woman, or the Family? Had they wiped his memories of them? Were his feelings artificial?

His mother didn't respond. She knew that he knew.

"Please, Gerry. Do this one thing. Find Petal and then come home to us. You belong here. We've missed you so much."

"What about Jasper? Did you love him too?"

She took a deep breath and tried to hide the hurt that

was still so clear on her face.

"I won't lie. I adored him. Though he didn't have your empathy, he had such a drive to live, and live in the right way. It hurts me deeply to see how quickly he changed, how far Seca drove him once he got his poisonous claws into him. I don't blame you for what you did. You had to do it."

"Where were you and all your resources while I was down there dying?"

"We were blocked," she said, sitting down on the edge of the bed. "Something jammed our communications and satellites. We tried to send help, but we couldn't get there soon enough. By the time the shuttle landed and the security team got to you, the rest of Jasper's allies had escaped. But you, Gerry. You saved the Dome. Saved everyone."

She leant over and kissed him on the cheek. His skin was still sore from the wounds.

Sighing, he sat up, sending the cat scooting off the bed.

"I'll do it. I'll find Petal. But let me make it clear. I'm doing it for me."

She closed her eyes and breathed out with relief.

"I want you to tell me one thing, though," Gerry said, scrutinising the woman, trying to divine any sense of deception.

"Anything."

"Tell me why you faked my life. Why the false memories? Why wasn't I told what I could do? That I was one with my AIA?"

"It was your father, Nolan's choice. He wanted you to stand on your own two feet. He wanted to give you the closest to a normal upbringing as possible."

"You think any life down there is normal?"

Amma shrugged. "It's as close to normal as we can get it."

Gerry shook his head and realised she didn't truly understand what it was like to be controlled, to live in fear of the D-Lottery. But she continued on, making her case.

"Your foster parents were real. Normal. They loved you as much as we do, and we entrusted them with your education. You had the benefit of knowing what it was to be like the others, but also, now, what it's like to be something else, something better. And it's that experience which makes you perfect for recovering Petal.

"It's not easy for me to let you go again. I've been watching you grow and develop for years and become the man you are, yet I couldn't speak with you, hold you. You talk of torture. It was torture for us watching you from a distance, always in fragments. But I couldn't interfere with your development. You needed time to find out what you were naturally.

"When you go for Petal, you'll have help. You won't be alone. We have a contact on the ground who will supply you with resources. You've met her."

"Enna?" Gerry asked.

"Yes. She's one of ours. Your aunt, in fact."

"So that's why she wanted me to take care of Petal... She knew what she was and knew you wanted her up here. Why didn't she say anything?" The clarity of truth just didn't jibe with what he got from Enna on the surface. He just couldn't see her as one of them. But if what Amma was saying was true, then he was one of them too. It made him sick. After everything he had learned about the Family, about the results of their weapons and actions, it turned out that all along he was another one of their number.

He shook his head. "None of this can be happening. None of this is real. How can I trust any of it?"

"We'll show you. And then you'll know the truth of who you are."

"Show me, then," he said, sitting up in the bed.

Amma held up a hand. "Easy, you're still recovering. Maybe tomorrow. Your full recovery might take a while."

"The more time I spend up here in your space station, the less time I'm on Earth finding Petal. Besides," Gerry said, "if she's so special to you, why don't you send a squad down there after her?"

"It's a question of resource management. And you really are best suited to the job. Besides, Enna's on the ground, tracking her. She has resources to do part of the job, but we'll need you to convince her to come back with you."

"And what makes you think I'll do that?" Gerry asked. "I'm not even convinced myself."

"That's what the next week or so is for. We'll convince you."

It sounded like a threat, such was the steel in her voice. Perhaps he was getting to the heart of her true nature. "Fine," Gerry said. "Either way, I will gladly return to the surface and find her."

He didn't mention that he'd bring her back. Finding her was priority number one. Anything after that wasn't as important. His mother hugged him, and he grudgingly gave in. The need for love and family floated like shallow oil on top of an ocean of hate for what they had done. The fact both Seca and Jasper had betrayed them was enough for Gerry to be wary of their intentions.

Although he had only been with Petal for a few days, he already felt close to her like she was his family. A desire to protect her burned deep. He would follow this woman's lead for now, gather intel, and then make sure no one would use or abuse Petal again.

***

Gerry finished his basic physiotherapy within his recovery room. Two days had passed since his surgery. He felt his body begin to recover, although it would take longer for him to return to his previous levels of fitness. Muscles, bones, and tendons clicked and popped as he put himself through the callisthenic exercises. Taking a deep breath to let his heart rate drop, he sat down on an armchair, and his hand naturally went to his head again.

They had given him a prosthetic, cybernetic eye replacement with the promise of enhanced vision and various recording and augmented overlay functions, but it wasn't hooked up to his internal systems yet. It felt wrong in his skull. Too heavy. He couldn't stop poking it through his skin, feeling the hard metal casing against his fingers.

During the last two days, he'd been given a nutrient-rich drip alongside real, cooked food. Despite himself, he grew accustomed to the luxury, reverting back to his old way of life, but throughout, he played the game, kept them onside, all the while observing them, learning from them. So far they'd kept their cards close to their chest. Both Amma and her precious, and arrogant, son, Tyronius, had treated him well; the latter talking Gerry through some of the systems of the station and some of the advancements he oversaw for their various transhuman and posthuman technologies.

It was clear to him, however, they weren't showing him everything; they soon diverted the subject and his attentions whenever he got too close to the details.

The station itself seemed to stretch for miles. Hallways and corridors without end, rooms and labs filled with computers, holoscreens, and busy men and women. They let him wander how he liked, although there were certain parts of the station locked down to him, despite the sound of activity beyond the various doors, making him wonder what they were doing, what they were building.

One of the busiest zones was the shuttle dock. He observed that once a day, a shuttle would leave the station for Earth, and another would return. The first one, they told him, was taking down a number of new officials to take over the running of Cemprom and the presidency.

It seemed Kuznetski had seen the end of his reign, although what had happened to him, Gerry could only speculate. Yet another detail they obfuscated.

Throughout his meanderings up and down the white-surfaced corridors, he struggled to catch on to any networks with his implant or his internal transceiver. He knew the station had incredible computation power both internally and externally with the Family's various satellites, but he could find no way in. They did a fine job of securing their systems.

He knew why—their head of IT: Jachz. A formidable example of the Family's technology.

It was 09:00 on the third day when Amma entered the

sparsely decorated recuperation room. Beige walls, white furniture—a bed, a cabinet, and a holoscreen stand—and a number of modern art pictures created with fractal calculations, made up the full complement of decor.

A tall, lithe man, wearing a sharply tailored grey suit, stood behind her. He was completely bald, with small, green eyes. They darted too fast, too precise. His movements were smooth, efficient, and without flaw as if he were made of liquid metal.

"Let me introduce you to your recovery manager," Amma said, standing aside and placing her hand on the man's arm. "Jachz will complete your systems upgrades and make sure you're ready for action."

Gerry stood and approached the man, although he knew the word man wasn't entirely accurate. He held out his hand. Jachz took it with a dry, cold grip. Squeezing just a little, Gerry noticed the lack of pulse. Unsurprising.

Given Enna had specialised in building transcendents—AI-controlled humanlike bodies—Jachz was no surprise.

"AI?" Gerry asked, eyeing Amma.

"Our finest," she said, her body puffing up with pride.

"Thank you," Jachz said. "I'm honoured to meet you, Gerry. I've heard a lot about you."

"Oh?" Gerry asked. "You'll have to fill me in on the details. It seems I don't know myself half as well as you all do." He meant to say it as a light-hearted quip, but the truth of his conviction came out, giving the words a knife edge.

Jachz closed his eyes for a second and inclined his head in respect. "I'll do my best to serve your recovery, Gerry. If you would like to come with me to my lab, we'll start our work. We have a number of challenges ahead of us."

"And maybe you can finally give me some answers," Gerry said.

"I will try my best."

Chapter 22

The recovery with Jachz took eight days in total. By the end, Gerry felt as if his mind had been processed over and over until all the kinks were planed smooth. His vision returned fully with the aid of his cybernetic replacement. It boasted a new feature: an AO—augmented overlay. A HUD display delivered various statistics and information provided by his AIA, which Jachz had reprogrammed to be faster and closer integrated with Gerry's unique brain.

"Tell me, then, Jachz," Gerry said while his brain was hooked up to Jachz's diagnostic and reprogramming system. "What exactly is it that makes my brain unique? Enna mentioned that I had another being within my subconscious."

Jachz sat on a stool in front of the holoscreen that stretched half the width of the six-metre-wide room. The whiteness of the walls and the semi-translucent blue hue of the screen gave Jachz's complexion a cold look. "That's not quite accurate," he said, turning to face Gerry, who was sat on a recliner with various cables running from his neck port into Jachz's system. "You have a secondary process running within your neural network."

"What does that actually mean?" Gerry asked, sitting

up. "How did that even occur?"

"It was Nolan, your father, who invented the idea. He created software that could run in the brain. Nanotechnology. Each tiny nano gate would connect with each other, bridging connections with your brain, creating a new kind of brain network—a logical computer. It allows your mind to work on two levels. That is the reason why you and your AIA, courtesy of the dermal chip, are so entwined. So much so that if we were to remove that chip, you would suffer considerable brain damage."

"So I am one with it all, then? Me, Mags, and this other nano network are all essentially... me?"

Jachz's face approximated a smile. The muscles were a little stiff compared to Enna's transcendents. Perhaps he didn't smile much in his day-to-day duties on the station.

"Yes," Jachz said. "They are as much you as your heart or your blood."

"And that's why I can create code in my mind? Why I can get into computer systems as easy as if I were breathing?"

Jachz inclined his head. That seemed to be his way of agreeing. His facial expressions never really changed much, so Gerry had to try to discern most of the meaning from his non-inflected speech and body language. "Tell me, Jachz, what makes you, you?"

"Can you be more specific?"

"I mean, you're an artificial intelligence controlling a physical, humanlike body. How does that work exactly? Do you have an organic brain? Are you like Enna's transcendents?"

"I regret to say I'm not completely aware of Enna's work,

but from the information I have been privy to, I would say we are similar in some aspects."

"What's the difference?" Gerry asked.

"I believe they are programmed to work within certain parameters. They are personality stereotypes that Enna has created. Although they control their bodies in much the same way as I do: a software-to-neuronal interface that translates thought to nerve information and thus muscle information, I have the capacity to learn and evolve, with one exception."

"And that is?"

"I am unable to feel or emote. I can approximate them. I am aware of appropriate responses, but they do not come naturally as they would to a human. Even Enna's creations are programmed to feel certain emotions. One of her early models was made to feel love and affection, for example."

"Do you wish you could feel?" Gerry asked.

Jachz blinked once and became still; so still that Gerry had a strange idea he might have perhaps crashed and was in need of a reboot. Shifting his legs off the recliner, Gerry made to move closer when Jachz's green eyes suddenly glowed and he became animate again.

"I can't answer that, as I know not what I miss. One cannot wish for something one does not know or understand."

"I suppose not," Gerry said, sitting back on the recliner. "Are we nearly done?" Streams of code continued to race down the giant holoscreen in front of Jachz, whose smooth gesturing and programming would occasionally cause a ripple among the code.

Internally, Gerry's thoughts quickened and sharpened

to the levels before his temporary death.

"Almost," Jachz said. "A few more minutes while I make sure your nano network is fully operational. It took a lot of damage, but I've repaired the majority of bugs and broken code. I just need to make sure it is working within the right parameters."

"What happens if it isn't?"

"It could overload your brain and damage cells. At the other end of the spectrum, it could retard your capacity to form memories or learn. It's a fine balance, but we're nearly there. Now, if you would just relax and clear your mind, I'll run the last of the diagnostics, and then we can run you through some final tests to ensure you are correct and fully functional."

"You make me sound like a robot," Gerry said.

"You are, Gerry. All humans are basically machines, after all. You are just a different kind of machine. One more capable than most. Now, please concentrate your mind, relax, and clear yourself of any thoughts. Especially any that cause distress. Those will only prolong this procedure."

Gerry sat back on the recliner and closed his eyes. At first he could think of no way to calm his mind as hundreds of questions came to him, begging for answers, but one by one he let them go until his consciousness focused on the image that had pervaded his thoughts since he came to the station. From within his recovery room, a porthole allowed him a partial view of space and the great blue marble that was Earth arcing across the aperture.

He fixed that image in his mind and let everything else go.

Jachz's procedural diagnostics caused a low-latency hum within Gerry's mind. It made his body tingle as if he'd been connected to a low-voltage battery. It helped him remain calm, like listening to white noise. As he fell ever deeper into a state of semi-unconsciousness, a state between waking and sleeping, he became aware of a dark shape lurking in the corners, just out of his full cognition.

It sat there, beckoning him to focus, to let his attentions go into the shadows of his mind. Curiosity took over, and being now more in the dream state, he let himself flow through the darkness towards this source of energy. For a brief moment the true scope of this other entity came into focus. Gerry reeled away as if from a monster in a nightmare. Black, infinite tendrils rushed to him, but Gerry was too quick.

He snapped his eyes open and exhaled a breath he had unknowingly held for too long. Dark blotches of colour covered his vision. He sat up and instinctively made to pull the cable from his neck port, wanting to get as far away from the black entity as possible. The glaring whiteness of the room soon cleared his vision and made him squint against the stark contrast.

"What the hell was that?" Gerry asked, thinking it was of Jachz's doing.

The AI leapt to his feet, bounded to Gerry, and prevented him from disconnecting the cable, grabbing his wrist with a fierce grip. "You must not do that, Gerry," Jachz said. "It'll damage the nano network. Please, just give it another minute to reboot, and we'll be done here."

Gerry's throat constricted. A pain throbbed within his head. "What did you do to me? What was that... thing in my head?" He could still see a shadow of the infinite tendrils reaching to him from the void of unconsciousness.

"I don't know what you mean," Jachz said, turning his attentions to the holoscreen. "I didn't do anything but run the various diagnostics. I could not make you see anything with this system. All this does is recalibrate your nano network. What did you see?"

The image had started to burn away by the fire of waking. Like a dream, it had vanished to some secret recess beyond his reach. The only evidence of any such thing was the feeling of dread and awe. Whatever it was, it had a vast intelligence. So very vast. "I can't describe it," Gerry said as the memory sped away from him faster than he could think.

"This is quite unusual. I see nothing in the log files to indicate unusual brain activity. This must be some artefact of the semi-dream state and the recalibration. I should notify the others."

Gerry grasped Jachz's arm. "No! You can't." He realised he was gripping Jachz tightly and eased the pressure. "Sorry, but I don't want anyone knowing about this. As you say, it's just a quirk. No more tests, no more diagnostics. I just want to go back to Earth. I'm done here. You understand?"

The AI paused for a moment, considering Gerry's words. Again, Gerry thought he had switched off such was his deathly stillness. Eventually he inclined his head. "I will finish here and let you be on your way, Gerry. There's no record of the incident, so I'll assume it's a human quirk."

"Thank you. I appreciate that."

With hindsight, Gerry would wish Jachz wasn't so

compliant.

***

The rest of the procedure went without incident. Jachz had mentioned a few times how impressed he was with Gerry's ability to recover and the capacity with which he could deal with complex programming problems. If Jachz had the ability to emote, Gerry was certain there would be an element of jealousy within his comments. But he couldn't feel and was merely making Gerry feel at ease.

When Jachz had finally finished and given Gerry a clean bill of health, he accompanied him to the shuttle bay ready for his return journey back to Earth. Within the dock of the bay, standing in a small group, his parents, Amma and Nolan, and his brother, Tyronius, along with Jachz and a number of engineers waited for Gerry to approach his shuttle.

A sleek two-seater craft, in the Family's colours of white and beige, shaped like a rounded wedge, awaited his boarding. A single gull-wing door hung open, showing him the sparse but comfortable interior. The journey would only take a couple of hours, but it was encouraging he would travel in comfort.

As he approached, Nolan stepped forward, his arms out wide as if waiting for a hug. Gerry stopped short. Throughout his stay, he'd only really interacted with Amma and Jachz, and occasionally the cold and distant Tyronius. Nolan had barely spoken with him during his recovery, but the way he acted as if he were saying goodbye to his best friend made Gerry only increase his disdain for his so-called father.

Realising Gerry wasn't going to reciprocate, Nolan dropped his arms by his sides and coughed to ease the embarrassment. The flashing blue and red docking lights of the shuttle bay created specular reflections on his bald head. His skin, the colour of polished mahogany, had a bright sheen to it. He fiddled with his round, silver-wire-rimmed spectacles, diverting his attention away from Gerry's gaze.

As much as he tried, Gerry could not return the warmth that Amma and Nolan had wished for. They might be his biological parents, and Tyronius, with his dark, slicked-back hair and sharp cruel features, might be his brother, but he looked on them as strangers, enemies even.

They had used Gerry, experimented on him and, despite bringing him back from death, only wanted him for what he could do, wanted him to bring Petal to them so they could continue with their experiments and advancements.

"Son?" Nolan finally said, stepping towards Gerry, gripping his arms. "I know none of this has been easy on you. I know you don't feel an emotional connection with us, but I want you to give us time. Try to see things from our perspective. When you come back with Petal, you'll have time to study us. Research our history, and then you'll understand why we did what we did, and why we do what we do. You and I are not so different."

"How's that?" Gerry asked, genuinely interested, especially as that last remark seemed to elicit a sneer from Tyronius, who stood next to Amma as if his very proximity would claim her as his own. As far as Gerry was concerned he was welcome to them.

"I hated my father too," Nolan said, releasing Gerry. "I hated what our great company had become at the time. Moving from environmental technology to that of an arms power. There's a blurring of lines when a corporation grows so powerful it becomes a sovereign entity in its own right."

"And yet you were still influential come the time this 'company' decided to end the war, and basically ended the world."

"Yes, but I was also the driving force, along with your mother, in rebuilding it. We gave humanity a future. Without us, there would be nothing." He sighed, letting his shoulders drop. "But I know this is an old conversation, and it'll never end. Such a massive event will always generate questions. But before you go, I want you to know that you will always have a place here with us, and that I hope when you return, you'll find it in yourself, even if it's just curiosity, to study with us, get to know us, learn the facts of this family, and then judge us."

"I will do that," Gerry said. "I believe that is only fair."

At that, Nolan smiled, and the tension of his body eased. Amma also smiled, her eyes showing it to be natural. Tyronius' sneer deepened.

"I'm pleased to hear it," Nolan said. "In the meantime, your new transceiver software will give you a direct connection to our communication satellite while on Earth. And your new eye will deliver us an audio and video feed, along with an augmented overlay to give you data during your mission. If there's anything you need while you're down there, or if you need to talk with any of us, we'll be here."

Gerry was already at work in deciphering the code that created that connection. When he got to the planet's surface, he had no intention of allowing that direct connection to continue. And he had no intentions of ever coming back and researching them.

He saw enough during his recovery. Saw the number of AI-controlled bodies being experimented on; saw how their coders were trying to come up with new types of intelligences, even devices in order to upload one's mind completely, which he had learned was Amma and Nolan's main line of interest. Immortality was their aim, one that was entirely posthuman and without the need for a body.

That was too far for him. Humanity was more than just a mind on a computer chip. Still, he continued the subterfuge, played the game, and made his way to the shuttle.

As he settled inside and the engineers got him set up, he turned to face the onlooking group. "I'll be sure to keep you updated on the status of my task."

"Safe journey, my love," Amma said. "And thank you. We look forward to welcoming you, and Petal, back to the station soon."

Gerry nodded and turned to the engineer. "I'm ready to go." The young woman in the grey coveralls radioed to the dock controllers and stood back from the shuttle as the door closed.

A voice came directly into Gerry's mind via his transceiver. "I'll be your liaison during the flight, Gerry," Jachz said. "Just relax and listen to my instructions, and you will be on the surface within a few hours. Are you ready?"

"Let's get this bird in the air, Jachz. I got a woman to find."

Chapter 23

The shuttle left the station with the grace of a swan. It pitched away in an arc towards Earth, leaving that great, long metal structure of the Family's home behind. For a moment Gerry held his breath at the majesty of space before him. Unlike being on the planet's surface, where pollution and clouds obscured the stars, here everything was sharp and clear and infinite. For the past couple of weeks he'd stared out of the porthole and watched the stars, but having this wider vista through the shuttle's holoscreen, he felt like he was right in the middle of a great void.

Jachz's instructions had finished. Gerry was told he would be flying silent for the next hour, unless he required anything. But he didn't. All he wanted was the quiet to enjoy the awe-inspiring views. It also brought into perspective the significance, or lack of it, of his life.

Out there on an endless number of worlds there must be other life, other people, creatures, types of life forms, all thinking they matter. But individually, they, including himself, those on the station, and those on Earth, amounted to so little. And yet that smallness mattered so much. A tiny blip of life on a dust fragment spinning through space had all the meaning in the universe.

It was during that journey towards the planet that he realised just how much he missed Petal. She'd sacrificed so much for him and kept him alive in numerous situations. There was no way he could betray that loyalty, or his feelings for her, by returning to the Family.

His mind was still at work unpicking the code that made up the connection to the Family's communication satellite. They had a whole collection of them in a low-earth orbit, providing various functions. It was the largest network he'd ever seen.

Despite his skills and his recovery, he couldn't get into the code, but he could at least program a roadblock to prevent them spying on him from within. As he sent his mind more fully into the communications satellite, he discovered a flow of data from a specific node. He guessed that was the satellite. It appeared to him as a massive data store, with other stores connected to it.

Unable to resist looking closer, he dove further in and analysed the data.

Within a split-second he knew it was a mistake.

His entire body tensed, and a deathly chill shrouded his soul. A force gripped his mind and dragged him further in.

The tendrils, he thought. A flash of code came to him, paralysing, probing. He tried to leave the data stream, bring his mind back to his body, but it was too late. The entity he'd briefly seen during his diagnostic approached. A massive, dark intelligence reached out to him.

Gerry screamed, squeezed his eyes shut, and spun a set of defensive code patterns. The entity swatted them away as if they were harmless flies. To Gerry's horror, he was aware of a change in the trajectory of the shuttle. Snapping his eyes open, still half in that data-state, he saw the Earth spinning away from him, to be replaced with the darkness of deep space.

The arcing stars caused a blurring flash before the shuttle stopped its change of direction. The thrusters engaged and sent him hurtling away from Earth, away from the Family's station. And worse: his communications were down.

The shuttles controls wouldn't respond. Even his desire to scream had been covered in an all-encompassing blanket of darkness as the great entity wrapped its digital will around Gerry's mind.

The station and Earth shrank behind him as he continued to hurtle into deep space. He let out a silent scream and battled to free his mind. A new enemy had found him.

Reborn, but under threat, Gerry once more faced a fight for survival.

The End.

Find Out What Happens Next

Get the next book in the series: Assembly Code (Book 2 of The Techxorcist) in either paperback or ebook formats:

US: http://www.amazon.com/dp/B00FH5ZPRG/

UK: http://www.amazon.co.uk/dp/B00FH5ZPRG

Join The Newsletter

Want to get the early scoop on my books and other material? Sign up to the newsletter and get exclusive content only available to newsletter fans. Join and receive:

* Previews of upcoming material
* Exclusive sample chapters and excerpts
* Free short stories
* Links to discounts and promotions before anyone else
* A chance to be a beta reader
* Access to early advanced reader copies in exchange for a fair review
* No spam. I only email you when there's something good to share.

Join Today!
http://eepurl.com/rFAtL

About The Author

Colin F. Barnes is a full-time writer of science fiction and thrillers. He's a member of both the British Fantasy Society and the British Science Fiction Association. He honed his craft with the London School of Journalism and the Open University (BA, English).

Colin has run a number of tech-based businesses, worked in rat-infested workshops, and scoured the back streets of London looking for characters and stories—which he found in abundance. He has a number of publishing credits with stories alongside authors such as: Brian Lumley, Ramsey Campbell, and Graham Masterton. He lives alone with a black cat in Essex in the UK. Rumours that the cat is the one with the talent is a malicious slur.

You can connect with Colin at the following places:

Website: www.colinfbarnes.com
Newsletter: http://eepurl.com/rFAtL
Twitter: https://twitter.com/ColinFBarnes
Goodreads: http://bit.ly/13uTiEx
Facebook: http://on.fb.me/16QW0lR

Acknowledgments

A big thanks to Krista Walsh, Tony Lane, Paul Holmes, Dave Robison, Gary Bonn, and Aaron Sikes for being generous and awesome.

33597283R00148

Made in the USA
Lexington, KY
01 July 2014